RESONANCE

THE WHISPERS OF RINGS COLLECTION

WRITTEN BY CATHERINE LACROIX
ARTWORK BY MARLENA MOZGAWA

BOOKS IN THIS SERIES:

WHISPER
PROMISE
ECHO
OATH
SILENCE

Tese L'etai,

Catherine LaCroix

Copyright ©2017 Catherine LaCroix
ISBN 9781974087631

LaCroix Publishing
www.whispersfromcat.wordpress.com

For Eunice and Eugene
Forever my favorite love story

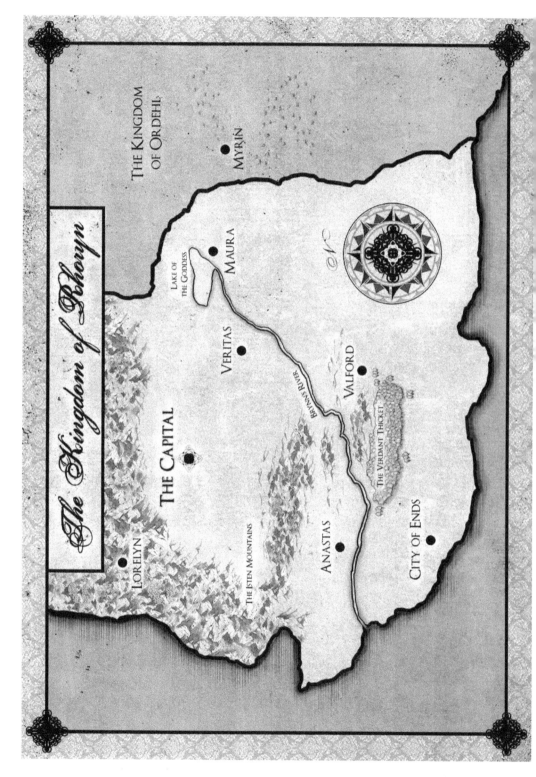

The Kingdom of Pchoryn

THE KINGDOM OF ORDEHL

MYRIN

MAURA

LAKE OF THE GODDESS

VERITAS

VALFORD

THE VERDANT THICKET

BRYNN'S REACH

THE CAPITAL

LORELYN

THE ISTEN MOUNTAINS

ANASTAS

CITY OF ENDS

I

The Temple of Elwyn housed the coldest, dankest cells I ever had the misfortune of spending time in.

A few other chambers at least afforded the luxury of a torch and a bedroll, but the guards spared me no such kindness. This wasn't the first time I found myself shackled to a wall, but it was never before under the pretense of murder. Generally, the public prison was found suitable enough for felons of the great city of Anastas. But according to the Elwyn clerics, only the best-guarded dungeon would do for a Whisper like me.

I couldn't remember how many days had passed since they dragged me from my home and locked me in. After three, I lost the ability to keep track of time; the guards kept unpredictable shifts, and windows were a comfort long forgotten. Even sleep refused to keep me company. The brutal nightmares tortured me to consciousness. My body succumbed to exhaustion only once—I awoke to a guard shaking me while demanding I stop screaming.

Food was another fond memory; I had nothing to eat from the first day of my imprisonment. Not only did they not bother offering sustenance, I heard it was common for the Temple to poison its occupants before any official judgment was made. The fewer mouths for them to feed the better.

"Still alive, wisp?" The most recent guard on duty raked his pike against the bars.

I didn't want to respond. My mouth was parched and my patience already long since evaporated. The King's Guard devised the term 'wisp' after Whispers became a despised race. A wisp;

only a shred, barely human. It was disgusting what they thought of me. All for things beyond my control.

"Answer me!" He didn't wait long before slamming his weapon once more against the door, startling the few other inmates.

"Unfortunately." The truth was bitter to taste.

There was nothing left for me. The damp floor soaked through my thin clothing, the cold air took every last drop of energy I hoped to preserve, and the metal that surrounded my wrists and ankles chafed my skin until it bled. I wanted to die.

"My lord, wait!" a voice called out. Heavy footsteps echoed from further down the hall, breaking the awkward silence between the guard and I. Visitors weren't common in the Temple dungeon. I strained to look into the darkness without much luck.

"You will give her to me and ask no further questions."

"But her trial! She must be judged!"

"I will pay any amount that you wish. Give it to the king, use it for this god-forsaken Temple, I don't care. You will hand her over to me immediately." The footsteps stopped abruptly and a tall, strong silhouette of a man appeared before my cell.

The few available torches didn't emit enough light for me to see his face. A second pair of feet scuttled quickly to rest beside him. The distant fire glinted off of the gold medallion that signified the cleric's power within the Temple.

"Josselyn Thorn?" The visitor's voice was soft, the most gracious gesture anyone had shown me since I arrived.

"Yes, my lord." I decided that addressing him as the cleric did was the safest course of action.

"My lady, I need you to tell me if you were Jeremi and Victoria Terryn's Ring."

"Lord Markov!" The shock in the cleric's voice didn't surprise me. Rings were a sensitive subject within Anastas, and the houses of Elwyn believed them taboo.

I couldn't hold back the tears that overwhelmed my vision. Hearing their names again tore at my heart as painfully as when I found them dead.

"This woman murdered them. She couldn't have possibly been their R…Rin.."

"Do you dare not utter the word, Father?" I couldn't hide the rancor in my tone. Followers of Elwyn would never understand my relationship with the Terryns. "Yes, my lord. I was their Ring."

"Open this door, Father," Lord Markov ordered.

"But, my Lord—"

"I said open it!" His voice rang against every wall of the dungeon before echoing back a dozen times.

The cleric fiddled with his keys, finding the one to my cell after what seemed like an eternity. He rushed to my side and unlocked the irons holding me down. The fresh air against my open wounds stung like the fires of hell.

Lord Markov slipped one arm beneath my knees and the other behind my back before lifting me from the floor. I wanted to protest—I knew nothing of this man—but his warm body felt like heaven after days of freezing on the wet stone. The soft silks and linens of his clothing brushed against my bare skin.

"You have my place of residence. Send me the amount of her bail and it will be paid," he said sternly to the cleric.

"Y-yes, m'lord," the cleric stammered.

"Why take a worthless whore? You could 'ave a real lady," another prisoner cackled. Her long fingers circled the bars, black eyes glittering at Lord Markov.

"Hold your tongue, maggot!" The guard charged to watch her slammed his spear against the gates of her cell.

"Bitch is prolly diseased anyways," she muttered angrily, then cackled again.

I clutched the front of my savior's tunic with a shaking fist. The steady stream of abuse in the dungeon was commonplace, but a small, irrational part of me was terrified that Lord Markov would change his mind and put me back.

"Perhaps she would do better without her tongue," Lord Markov growled.

"I'm sorry, m'lord. She doesn't know who she's speaking to." The cleric dabbed a cloth against his forehead. I could see his trembling hands in the dim lighting.

"Then educate her."

With his final retort, Lord Markov carried me through the dungeon and into the Temple's main hall. Extravagant rugs of red and gold lined the floors beneath rows of seating. Golden, winged beings watched over their followers from high on the walls. At the head of the Temple was a giant ivory statue of Elwyn herself; a lovely maiden with stargazer lilies weaved into her flowing hair. According to the stories, her death put an end to a thousand year war. As I didn't practice religion, I only picked up bits and pieces from her followers. I did hear it told more than once that Elwyn was also a Whisper, but it was never depicted in her paintings. It was an idea I enjoyed entertaining while I wasted away in that cell. People such as myself would be treated quite differently if the martyr of their religion were one of us.

As quickly as we entered the Temple hall, we were rid of it, stepping into the morning sun. I hadn't realized how much I had adjusted to the darkness of my cell until the glaring sunlight rendered my vision useless.

"So the rumors were true, then. You are a Whisper." He spoke to me carefully, as if his words would break me apart.

"Do you now think me a diseased whore?"

"I wouldn't give a large portion of my investments to a useless temple for a diseased whore."

I leaned my head into his chest and closed my eyes. With the warmth of the sun and the smooth rhythm of his steps, it was hard not to drift off to sleep. The sound of Anastas' citizens preparing for the day was a comfort I'd taken for granted.

"I thank you for not referring to me as a wisp," I murmured.

"Your kind are far too beautiful to merit such a disgraceful title." His voice was like velvet, caressing my every nerve.

That voice alone brought the heat back into my freezing limbs. I felt color rise to my cheeks.

The basic features of my race are impossible to hide; shocking white hair, caramel skin, and eyes the color of frozen water. Men, even if their lineage wasn't immediately evident, could pass on the traits of Whispers to their children. Women born as Whispers would never continue the race; they were infertile. I was the end of my namesake.

The traits of a Whisper, however, aren't simply a thing of inheritance. Despite the drawbacks, all Whispers, men and women alike, harbor a menagerie of incredibly heightened senses. My blood incessantly runs hot with a desire not easily sated. My skin tingles and responds to even the slightest of touches. Unlike followers of the faith of Elwyn, I am free in my creed to love as I see fit.

I was the perfect Ring.

"Hold tight, now." Lord Markov gingerly placed me onto a cushion. I realized with increasing alarm that I knew nothing of this man. The cleric had regarded him as a Lord and the guard had demanded respect from the other prisoner, but what did that mean to me?

My panic eased as I remembered I was ready to die in that cell. What difference did it make if this man would kill me instead?

His touch disappeared and I was left only with the sensation of the soft fabric beneath me. I chanced to open my eyes and was happy to find my vision clear as the door closed beside me. I recognized that I was in a carriage, despite rarely having traveled in one. It was large enough for four and I felt embarrassingly small sitting alone inside it.

"Let's go home, Sam." I heard Lord Markov's voice muffled through the walls before he opened the door on the opposite end.

He climbed into the carriage beside me. Upon studying his face, my heart skipped a beat.

He could have been Jeremi Terryn's twin. The silver eyes that glittered in a way that made me catch my breath when he smiled. The same dark, silken hair that begged for fingers to stroke through each strand, high cheekbones that softened his angular features. I struggled to find words as my stomach tied itself into knots.

"Lord Markov—"

"Please, call me Adrien."

"Adrien… Who are you?"

"I'm Jeremi Terryn's brother. When I heard the news of his and Victoria's untimely passing, I came to Anastas as soon as I could. Jeremi wrote to me about you many times in our correspondence, but he and his lady wife kept you very well hidden."

"You don't share his name?"

"No, my lady. That is a story for another day."

It wasn't the first time I'd heard of someone changing their name to break family ties. I sifted through my exhausted thoughts to recall if Jeremi ever mentioned a brother. I came up with nothing. If Adrien would speak to me another day on the subject, I at least owed him that courtesy.

"How did you know about…their deaths?"

"I live in Valford, barely a day's ride from here. One of Jeremi's trusted servants had a letter in my hands the next morning. She mentioned you were locked away as you were found in their room with the bodies."

No one believed me when I told them the truth; I found them murdered in their bed. I was the only possible suspect according to the guards that found me. Not only was I Jeremi and Victoria's Ring for three years, I was also in their servitude for nearly ten. That meant nothing to the masses of Anastas.

"Adrien, do you think I killed them?"

He paused for a time. I shifted uncomfortably in my seat as I tried to keep my eyes on him. The resemblance to Jeremi was eerie and my emotions weren't prepared to handle it. After studying me carefully, he took my left hand. He massaged my ring finger, where a small, intricate tattoo encircled the base.

"No, I don't think you killed them. I don't believe you had any motive to. The position of a Ring is one held in high regard, especially if a Whisper obtains it."

Rings were becoming more of a common occurrence in a married household. They were considered a link between a man and wife: a person that would satisfy a couple's every need whether on an emotional or physical level. I knew the Terryns better than any person alive and they treated me like a queen. I'd lived with them, dined with them, reveled in their joys, and shared their bed when they beckoned. They'd housed me, clothed me, showered me with a wealth I'd never known or needed, and loved me as I'd loved them. I missed them so much…

"Josselyn, are you alright?"

I didn't realize I was crying until Adrien called my name. I wiped my eyes on the inside of my arm, doing my best to not touch the expensive fabric of the carriage with my blackened hands. I was covered in grime from the cell from head to foot. I felt disgusting. I shook my head to clear thoughts of sleep—I still had more questions that needed answering.

Adrien fished a small cloth from inside his cloak and took one of my hands in his. With methodic strokes, he cleaned the dirt from my fingers. I couldn't remember the last time I was shown such a kindness. I watched him for a moment, collecting my thoughts.

"If they never mentioned that I was a Whisper, how did you find me?"

"I knew your name. A name stained with blood is not a well-kept secret."

"Pardon me if it is too bold, Adrien, but if you knew I was locked away, what took so long to find me?"

"The prison guards spoke as if you were already dead. No one wanted to admit the Temple took you until they had a respectable amount of gold in their pockets."

There wasn't going to be a trial. They were trying to kill me in that cell and claim it was suicide. I felt numb.

"Why did you come for me?" The question burned in the back of my mind since he set foot in front of my cage.

"In one of Jeremi's last letters I received, he asked me to take care of you and his wife should anything ever happen to him. I couldn't ignore my brother's last wish." He took my second hand and cleaned it with equal care as the first.

"So how do I repay you?"

"What do you mean?"

"Do you want me as a servant in your home? I feel I should repay you somehow for my life."

"Josselyn, I don't want you to work at my estate as a servant. I have enough of those. What I need is…something more." The smile that spread across his lips was all too familiar. I witnessed it on Jeremi's face so many times before.

I was suddenly curious as to what Jeremi wrote in his letters.

"I will feed you and clothe you, and you will want for nothing. I believe you have the correct set of skills to fulfill your part of the bargain."

In spite of the warm sun and the exhaustion that wracked my body, I felt a chill slide down my spine. I couldn't give credence to what Adrien was proposing; I was too hungry and too tired.

"We can talk about that when we arrive." He folded the dirtied cloth and set it aside before procuring a satchel from the carriage floor. He unwrapped it, revealing varied fruits, cheeses, and bread that set my mouth watering. I began to devour the small meal before he could place the cloth completely in my lap. Laughing, he handed me a skin of water. "Don't eat too quickly. It's not going anywhere."

I couldn't heed his words; my stomach was doing all of the thinking for me. As soon as I polished off the last breadcrumb and drained the skin to the last drop, exhaustion finally took me. I couldn't keep my eyes open and Adrien noticed.

"We'll be on the road for some time. You're welcome to sleep."

Without thinking, I glanced at Adrien's lap before my eyes flickered back to his face. The cushions would have served perfectly fine. The carriage was large enough to fit me comfortably if I curled my knees to my chest. Besides, I barely knew this man.

Even so, a knowing smile curved his lips and I felt a flush of embarrassment creep up my neck and paint my cheeks. He said nothing, only carefully guided my head onto his thigh and helped arrange my legs on the length of the seat. He stroked my head and the steady lull of the carriage rocked me like a cradle. For the first time in as long as I could remember, I fell into a dreamless sleep.

II

"We're here." Adrien's voice gently brought me back to awareness.

I realized the sun had already disappeared beneath the horizon and the moon served as our guiding light for some time. I felt refreshed and alert, but the gravity of my situation weighed heavily upon my heart.

Before I could consider what had transpired, Adrien pointed out the window and I followed his hand. "Welcome home, Josselyn."

I was speechless as I gazed at Adrien's abode. It was larger than the Terryns' estate, spanning nearly half an acre. Decorative lanterns hung from the hundreds of trees and plants that littered the front garden. Ivy wrapped around large columns that towered over the front doors. Four different pathways began near the road, leading to similar destinations after winding through the greenery. Alongside them, small water fountains bubbled merrily near stone benches.

"It's beautiful." I caught my breath. "Do you have a wife to share this with, Adrien?"

"No, my dear. I reside here alone with my servants."

I looked over the estate from top to bottom. It was stunning, more than I ever could have imagined. Yet…my heart yearned for the place I called home for so many years.

Adrien's words echoed back to me. *I need you for something more.*

"Lord Markov…do you understand what it means to be a Ring?"

He didn't speak as the carriage brought us closer to the stables. I resolved to continue.

"I was as loyal to the Terryns as they were to each other. One becomes a Ring until death. I was to take no one else as a lover, husband, or wife. As you are aware, I was claimed and it's not something I can remove—"

"Miss Thorn, excuse me by saying this but, what choice do you have left? Do you currently possess anything that would allow you to continue your life as their Ring?"

"The Temple took everything from me—"

"Except your life."

It was my turn to hold my tongue.

"Josselyn, I don't mean to be rude. But your loyalties can lie elsewhere. According to your own words, you're free of your commitment. 'Until death', you said. Allow yourself the time to heal."

"But the vows I took…" My words to Jeremi and Victoria were as set in stone as the ones they made to each other. I couldn't betray them.

"You're still young. Cutting yourself off from love is a rash decision that you're making too quickly. You are not a prisoner here. What you must understand is the rest of the world sees you as a murderer. I believe you deserve a second chance. Don't you?"

I couldn't respond. The words wouldn't come. He was right; he'd saved me from what was certain death and offered me almost everything I lost. I owed him my life and needed to consider his advice before condemning myself.

The carriage finally pulled into the stables and Adrien exited first, opening the door for me and offering his hand. "Can you walk?"

"Yes, thank you." My joints and muscles ached from so many days in that cell. The chill evening air burned against the raw, chafed skin of my wrists and ankles. Still, walking on my own was liberating.

The smooth cobblestone kissed my feet with each step. Mist from the fountains drifted on the breeze, cleansing my skin and sending a shiver down my spine. The stars smiled down from the dark heavens, welcoming me back to the world above the Temple dungeons. I was free.

Adrien led me through a small section of his gardens to the front door. Three servants greeted us, all wearing warm smiles and matching clothing; long, dark skirts and fitted bodices the color of deep red wine. Their hair was tied back into varying styles away from their faces.

"Girls, would you be so kind as to show Lady Thorn to her chambers and ready her bath?"

"Of course, m'lord." They bowed in unison—a little disconcerting—before taking my arms and leading me through the many halls.

We arrived in a luxurious room that took me by surprise. A large bed was positioned against the wall with a canopy draped in silks, adjacent to a cheery, crackling fireplace. Near the door was an intricately carved vanity the color of ivory. A door against the far wall led into what I assumed was a large wardrobe, but the lamp's light didn't illuminate that far. One servant stayed to help me undress from my prison rags while the other two drew hot water into an ebony tub.

"Remarkable...I've never seen a Whisper in person." The woman undressing me admired my skin and touched my hair. Even though I was covered in prison grime, she viewed me as something extraordinary.

Accepting compliments was not my forte. I had grown accustomed to the constant admiration of gawkers as much as I had the slander. I remained silent as she led me to the bath.

The other two servants joined the first and went to work scrubbing every inch of my skin. The water was scalding hot, just as I'd always enjoyed it. One young girl set to brushing the many tangles out of my hair, which was a feat in itself. I bit my lip in an effort to stifle my protests when she caught the comb against a knotted mass. The wet floor of the Temple hadn't done me any favors. The Terryns had pleaded with me to never have my hair cut, leaving me with a waist length mane that fought back as if it had a mind of its own.

It felt amazing to be clean again, and the chill finally evaporated from my bones. After assisting me from the bath and toweling me dry, they dabbed my now shimmering hair and throat with oils that smelled of roses and lilacs. One servant brought in a container of salve that was spread around my wrists and ankles. The lotion soothed the fire of my shackle wounds. For the first time in days, I felt like I'd gained back one small piece of myself.

"Girls, please excuse us." Adrien entered without warning.

"Of course, m'lord." The servant girls bowed and left me standing naked in the middle of the room.

I cursed them silently for taking the towel with them. I swore I could hear one of them giggle as she took her leave.

"Please, pardon my intrusion." The look in his eyes said he was anything but sorry.

"Adrien…" I quickly turned away from his gaze, covering myself as best I could with my hands. I was terrified of disappointing him—it meant the difference between living in his luxury and returning to that horrible dungeon.

"Let me see you." It was a command, not a question.

Slowly, I turned to face him and let my arms fall to my sides.

"Beautiful." He bridged the gap between us in a few large, deliberate steps. His warm hands caressed my face and hair, slowly moving to my shoulders.

"My lord—" I wasn't mentally ready for what he wanted, yet my body yearned for him desperately.

"Jeremi and Victoria were very lucky indeed," he purred as his hands wandered further south to stroke my breasts.

His delicate touch rekindled a heat that lay dormant in my blood. Standing there vulnerable in front of him felt... right. Almost familiar. Although, somewhere deep within my rational thoughts was a voice that screamed I stop, it was buried deep beneath the cravings that overtook me with each stroke of his fingers.

Unfortunately, what my desires begged of me, my body could not handle. My knees trembled for the span of a few heartbeats before I felt myself falling.

"Josselyn!" Adrien's arms were there to catch me before I hit the ground.

"I-I'm sorry, Adrien. I—"

"You need rest. We'll have all the time in the world, my sweet." He brushed the loose strands of hair away from my face. "I shouldn't have acted so quickly."

I felt embarrassed, ashamed, weak. I was terrified of disappointing him, my skin yearned for the pleasure of his fingers, yet my muscles ached for rest.

He carefully guided me to bed and pulled down the covers for me. I crawled beneath the blankets and he tucked them tightly around me once I'd settled in. My eyelids were heavy with exhaustion, and still I clung to Adrien's hand. I didn't want to go back to the temple's dungeons. I couldn't handle the City of Ends again. I'd rather die.

"I can't…go back," I murmured, unable to stop the tears that plagued me. "I can't…"

"Josselyn, you aren't going anywhere," he whispered. Running his hand through my hair, he kissed the top of my head. "I promise you."

I wanted to say more, to speak the hundreds of fears that plagued me. But the warmth of the fire, the comfort of a real bed…I felt myself drifting off.

"I'll be here when you wake up," he assured me.

Moments later, I knew no more of the world.

Awareness returned to me in slow waves. The soft blankets caressing my skin, the comfort of a crackling fire, the last glitters of sunset, and finally Adrien, seated leaning against the vanity with a book in his hand. I studied him carefully, astonished by features that were so similar to Jeremi's. Even the gentle curve of his lips mirrored those of his brother.

"Ah, you're awake." His silver eyes met mine as a smile played at his lips.

I nodded and stretched, my joints aching from lack of movement.

"How long was I asleep?" I asked, almost fearing the answer.

"Two days, but you've clearly needed it." Placing the book on the vanity, he lifted a tray and goblet, carrying them to where I lay. "I can only imagine you're hungry."

"Two days…Seven hells. Adrien, forgive me."

"For what?" Easing himself beside me, he placed the tray on my lap. A variety of fruits, meats, breads, and cheeses lay sprawled in front of me. I couldn't help myself, I began eating immediately.

"Two days?" I asked between mouthfuls. "Why didn't you wake me?"

"You were in that dungeon for eight days. With the rumors I've heard of the generous Temple of Anastas, I can only assume without food, water, or sleep."

I took a sip from the water filled goblet. The familiar sensation of dehydration still ravaged my throat.

"I'd much rather you feel at your best," he continued.

I met his gaze and shivered. Yes, I could only imagine how much he yearned to see me at peak performance.

"Can you stand?" He moved the empty platter back to the vanity and stood before the fireplace with his arms crossed.

I slipped from the bed, the heat of the flames warming my bare skin. My steps were sure and balanced, my head was absent of the vertigo that felt like second nature. I felt like myself again.

"Good girl." Adrien stepped forward to meet me, his voice low and alluring. My breathing caught with his words.

When mere inches separated us, he leaned toward me, shifting my hair behind my ear and holding my face in his hand.

"May I?" It was barely a whisper in my ear, but my heart set to racing at his warm breath against my skin.

"Yes," I murmured. I grasped at his tunic and pressed myself against him.

With fire lighting his silver eyes and a devilish smile on his lips, Adrien knelt and teased my breast with tiny bites. I moaned and found myself grabbing handfuls of his soft hair in an attempt to push his teasing further. He laughed under his breath before his mouth encompassed my nipple and his tongue massaged it furiously.

Every single nerve in my body stood on end. His fingertips moved to lightly brush my inner thighs while he continued to work his tongue. One hand ventured north and parted my folds easily, his fingers slipping inside me without any resistance. We gasped in unison.

"You're already dripping," he murmured against my skin, his tongue moving from breast to navel. I shuddered as his searing hot breath traveled gradually down my stomach.

Every touch, caress, and bite was amplified ten times and brought me to the edge.

"Adrien." His name entwined itself into my breathing.

"I'd heard stories about Whispers, but never expected this," he muttered.

My hips moved in rhythm as he worked his fingers in and out of me at a speed that promised I would climax soon.

"Don't hold back on me," he commanded.

Words evaded me. Pleading whimpers were all that would form on my lips.

Adrien traced a small circle around my navel with his tongue before sliding to my hip. Then dangerously close to his occupied hand. I could hardly draw breath. My heart skipped beats. His left hand cupped the small of my back and he guided my quivering body to the floor. The plush rug caressed my bare skin like a thousand soft kisses. He traced my hip bone before sinking his teeth into the tender flesh. Air hissed through my teeth. My hands desperately searched for purchase. I settled on the long fibers of the rug and gripped them until my knuckles turned white. So many intoxicating sensations combined were enough to drive me mad.

"Patience, little one." His breath tickled the taut curve of my stomach and I thrust my hips toward his tongue.

"Please," I gasped. More fingers filled me and continued his maddening pace. I could feel the tension quickly building inside of me.

"But what of your Ring?"

For the span of a heartbeat, I ceased to feel his mouth or his fingers. I looked at him, past the features that reminded me so much of Jeremi, and I saw only Adrien. I could read the intense hunger in his eyes, and it set my heart aflame. If this was what he wanted in return for my life, I'd give it.

"Take me, Adrien," I whispered. "Please…"

"As you wish." With a wicked smile, he spread my thighs with his free hand. His mouth hovered just long enough to draw a whimper from me before finally reaching its destination. A cry that I'd suppressed since he'd begun teasing me tore from my throat as he stroked against the peak of my pleasure.

"I can't…hold it," I moaned.

He continued pumping his fingers and working his tongue, encouraging me to let go.

The first clenches of orgasm took hold moments later, and I squealed as waves of release rolled over me. Adrien pressed on. He applied more force with his tongue and plunged his fingers deeper, massaging the exact spot that extended my convulsions. The carnal sounds that escaped my lips only encouraged him, and I felt my eyes roll back. Pleasure completely erased my thoughts. My body involuntarily arched and eagerly responded to his every touch.

"Josselyn," I heard my name from somewhere far away. "You're incredible."

Adrien pulled his fingers from me, leaving an aching void. He moved to unhook and discard his trousers. My own hands searched out his tunic and forced it over his head. His body showed signs of many hours of physical labor and my eyes widened when my gaze landed on his erect manhood. I felt any remaining body heat flow between my thighs as I wrapped my own legs around his lower back. I pulled him in toward me.

"Take me as long as you wish," I begged.

He thrust into me without mercy while my hips responded in kind. Another climax was building and I knew I wouldn't be able to hold back. My increasing cries of desperation said as much to Adrien.

"Come for me again," he whispered into my ear.

My teeth sank into his shoulder to muffle my screams, my entire body consumed with release.

"You feel amazing," I gasped, clawing my nails down his back.

He pulled away and placed his hands on my thighs, a smile tugging at the corner of his mouth when I moaned in protest.

"We're not done. Get on your knees," he instructed.

My thighs throbbed, the muscles unused for so long. I turned onto my hands and knees, gripping the rug. He angled my face closer to the ground, pulling my hips higher and leaving what he wanted completely vulnerable.

"Good girl," he growled and penetrated me from behind.

My hair spilled around my arms in a waterfall of silver. He reached for a fistful of the white pool and pulled, arching my back and exposing my throat. I dug my nails deep into the rug as my breathing turned shallow.

He grabbed my right hand and placed it between my legs, encouraging me to pleasure myself with my fingertips. Satisfied with the new position, he reached around to tease my hardened nipple.

"Again," he demanded. "Let me feel you come again."

Between his thrusting and our fingers, it wasn't long before I fulfilled his request. In the span of a few breaths, my whole body clenched in climax and I was shouting his name. Never was I allowed such ecstasy in that short amount of time. I'd lost control of my senses. All I wanted was him. Every part of him. Nothing else mattered. I pulled away slowly and my body still ached with yearning.

"Allow me," I purred, barely recognizing my own voice. Surprise toyed with his determined features as I turned to face him and pressed on his chest, pushing him to the floor. I positioned myself over him. "Just relax."

I guided him back inside of me, enjoying every inch. When at last my hips kissed his, a low groan escaped my throat. I moved at a pace to torture him, just as he'd done to me. His hands latched onto my hips, his fingers digging into my sides as he tried to take control of the situation. I wouldn't allow it. It was my turn. I continued at my own pace, drawing rasping moans from deep within his chest.

"You're an extraordinary creature—"

I thrust my hips down quickly, interrupting his thought.

"Come," I urged, leaning over him so our foreheads touched. "Don't think about anything else."

I pushed his wrists to the floor, forcing him to relinquish all control. Still, he fought to mediate the speed, but I would return to my original pace until he gave in and matched my tempo. I was approaching climax once more and was determined to wait for him.

"You're still so tight," he moaned, moving his body in sync with mine.

I worked him faster and his breathing accelerated. I let go of his wrists when I felt him nearing orgasm and he grasped my hips in desperation. He pushed into me faster than I could respond and I let him. His moans filled the room as he balanced dangerously on the edge.

"Come for me," I whispered.

Adrien cried out and thrust harder than he had yet. My thighs clenched around him as I bore down on him. I closed my eyes and experienced one last satisfying apex. As I descended from the high, I opened my eyes. I realized that my fingers were entwined with his and gave his hands a gentle squeeze. He was smiling, a mischievous smile that summoned chills and brought a heat that seemed to forever dwell in my soul to the surface of my skin.

"Oh, Josselyn," he murmured. "I've searched for you for a long time."

"And now you have me," I replied, returning his smile.

And he did.

III

I dreamt of Victoria that night. Gentle, breathtaking, Victoria. With sparkling sapphire eyes, fair skin, and almond hair that cascaded down her shoulders in a waterfall of loose ringlets. Lorelyn, the place she once called home, lay far to the northwest of Anastas, within the Isten Mountains. Jeremi met her on a business trip and they fell in love within the few days they spent together. Her beauty brought many a sidelong glance from the men of Anastas, but she only had eyes for Jeremi and me. I loved her with all of my heart.

My dream was of a nigh forgotten memory, safely tucked away in the depths of my mind.

Since the age of thirteen I'd served the Terryns; cooking, cleaning, tending to the gardens and responding to their every need. By my twenty-third nameday they'd given me my own room, supplied me with a full wardrobe, and many times invited me to share in their evening pleasures.

Mere months before I became their Ring, the summer's illness took its toll on the Terryn household. It put me in bed for six days that seemed never-ending. Victoria took it upon herself to care for me, and the tenderness she displayed only deepened my affections for her.

That particular evening, Victoria personally bathed and dressed me, and brewed a large mug of tea—aided with medicines from Jeremi—that soothed my constantly aching throat. I positioned myself atop soft pillows while she lounged close behind me, deftly plaiting my hair with practiced fingers.

"I wish I could braid as quickly as you can," I said longingly.

"We'll keep practicing once you are well." Everything she said sounded like a soft melody meant only for my ears. I never heard Victoria raise her voice in anger.

"Thank you for caring for me, my lady—"

"Victoria," she corrected patiently. "Josselyn, you are very important to Jeremi and I. We want you to feel at home."

"I've always been comfortable here." I took another sip of tea, struggling for more that I could say. Comfortable was an understatement. This *was* my home. There were a few beats of companionable silence while she separated another section of hair to braid.

"Do you think about your parents often?" she asked.

The question took me off guard. My family wasn't generally a topic of conversation.

"For a long time, I did," I answered. "Not anymore. I was worth more in gold than shared blood to them. I...I've long since let it go." I toyed with a loose thread on one of the cushions. "You and Jeremi are closer to me than my true family ever was."

Victoria tied off the end of her work and shifted around so we were face to face. She brushed a stray strand of hair from my cheek with cool fingertips and smiled, setting hundreds of butterflies free in my stomach.

"We will stay by your side always, my sweet. You should remember that." Clasping my free hand in her own, her demeanor was suddenly serious. "There are some very important things that Jeremi and I have been discussing recently. Soon, we may ask you to make a very personal decision. I want you to know that whatever your choice, we will still love you... Josselyn?"

I didn't understand the sudden droplets that fell on our clasped hands. Why was I crying?

"Josselyn?" The voice was no longer hers, yet still familiar. "Josselyn are you alright?"

One image blurred into the next as I regained consciousness. Adrien lay beside me, one arm beneath the pillow supporting my head. The other hand caressed my cheek, wiping away fresh tears.

"Adrien." A sharp pain in my chest labored my breathing.

"Shhh. It's alright, I'm right here." His lips brushed my forehead as I became increasingly cognizant of our naked bodies pressed together. "You were shaking so violently. Did you have a nightmare?"

"No. Victoria…She was…I…what have I done?" I'd betrayed them. I'd barely had time to mourn their deaths before I allowed another man to take me to bed. My vision blurred as the sobs built in the back of my throat.

"Let it out, love. Let yourself cry." He pulled me closer and I did just that. "You're safe here. Nothing can hurt you."

"I broke my vows. How could I?" I cried.

"Josselyn, you did no such thing." He stroked my hair and muttered words of comfort against my forehead.

We will stay by your side always. I clung to Adrien and allowed every heartbroken, bitter, angry, emotion I held since I'd discovered their bodies to take its time in my heart.

I wept myself numb and Adrien never left my side. His embrace had a grounding effect that reminded me why I'd allowed myself to let go. Eventually, my breathing evened and the tears stopped.

"I'm sorry…" I wiped my eyes and buried my face in his chest. "I didn't mean—"

"You have nothing to apologize for." He tipped my chin up, his gaze meeting mine. "Always apologizing, Lady Thorn. We'll break the habit yet. What do you say we share something to eat and I'll show you Valford?"

I smiled and nodded. I strongly believed that learning the city was the right step in making it feel like home.

"A smile suits you much better than tears, Josselyn." He kissed my forehead and moved from the bed to get dressed. "If you're alright with the clothes the girls here wear for now, we'll start refilling your wardrobe."

"Anything is better than that prison garb." I looked around the room to find the paper-thin white gown was gone. "Which, I hope you burned."

"Near enough," he laughed, fastening his tunic closed. He went to the wardrobe and returned in short time with a skirt and bodice identical to the servants' clothes. "These should fit for the time being."

I slipped from beneath the sheets and took the clothing from him. The fabrics were well weighted and finely woven. No expense spared even for his servants. As I slipped one leg into the skirt, the door to the bedroom opened.

"Adrien—" A young woman entered, dressed for travel. Long red curls framed her porcelain face. Emerald green eyes measured my naked body before returning to Adrien. "I wasn't aware you were hiring a...new girl."

"Isabelle, you're late," Adrien sighed. "I've told you when I need you here and it's not up for discussion."

"I'm...sorry, m'lord." Her perfect red lips pursed, her gaze digging into me.

I managed to slip into the skirt and was doing my best to string the bodice on my own.

"Don't let it happen again. I mean it," he reprimanded.

"Who is she?" Isabelle continued, her tone flat.

"My name is Josselyn Thorn. I'm—"

"A Whisper." The words were toxic on her tongue. She did nothing to hide her distaste.

"Isabelle," Adrien cautioned. "You will address Josselyn as if you're speaking to me."

Her eyes narrowed. "Is that so?"

"Lady Thorn will be living here from now on. You will attend to her every need. Do you understand me?"

I finished lacing the bodice and met Isabelle's cold eyes.

"Of course, m'lord." Her gaze remained steadily on me.

"Now, go get dressed and find Lily before she burns down the kitchen."

Isabelle took her leave without another word. A shiver ran through me. She was beautiful. She was breathtaking. She hated every fiber of my being.

"She barks worse than she bites. I'll make sure she minds her manners," Adrien said calmly.

"I'm sure she's just surprised," I said, despite the fact that I wasn't sure at all.

"You may be right. Nevertheless, perhaps we should find breakfast in the city." Adrien took my hand and led on to introduce me to Valford. To my new home.

IV

drien's estate was perched at the top of one of the many hills that carved the landscape of Valford. At the edge of the gardens, it was easy to see the lively city shops below. Smaller homes were scattered among the adjacent hills, before spilling into the streets surrounding the center of town. The carriage clattered along the winding road leading down into the main streets. Adrien had debunked my idea of walking the path—he claimed we would be lucky if the carriage fit my wardrobe alone—and I was not about to argue with him. Fall colors painted the many trees lining the roads and dotting the hills; oranges, yellows, reds. Time had escaped me. A gentle breeze danced through the foliage and played with loose strands of my hair. From the corner of my eye, I caught Adrien watching me with fascination.

The carriage came to a halt just on the outskirts of the busiest street. Adrien stepped out and before I could make a move to leave, the driver opened the door and extended a gloved hand toward me.

"My lady." He smiled.

"Thank you…Sam, was it?"

"Yes, my lady."

I took his hand and stepped down from my seat. Sam was a kind, cordial and well-spoken young man—very different from most men I met in my travels. His bright, tousled hair and tanned skin told of a childhood lived outdoors and I liked him better for it.

"We'll meet you back here in six hours, Sam." Adrien handed him a small purse that clanked with the familiar sound of coin. "Do as you wish until then."

"Thank you, Lord Markov." He bowed and led his horse by hand to a nearby stable.

"Now, where to begin." Adrien smiled and took my arm.

Already, passersby were risking glances in our direction, eyes widening at the sight of me. In Anastas, many of the townsfolk recognized me easily and didn't give a second thought to a Whisper with a prominent family. A majority of the people in Valford had likely never seen one of my race before—let alone accompanied by someone with such prestige.

"Don't worry about them." Noticing my worried glances, Adrien kissed my forehead. "No one will say anything while you're with me."

I nodded and we began to peruse the streets. The shop stalls I was accustomed to were replaced by well-kept buildings with beautiful storefronts covered in flowers and bright paints. Not one brick looked out of place in Valford's shopping district, and the same could be said for its attendees. Men and women both walked the roads in their best clothing—fine satins and velvets intricately embroidered with floral patterns in gold thread. Compared to their wardrobes, I felt plain in Adrien's servant dress.

"This way." He guided me through a door and as I took in the store I gasped.

Expensive clothing filled the room from top to bottom; one side for gentlemen, the other for ladies. Anything from traveling leathers to ball gowns was carefully displayed throughout their business.

"Lord Markov, welcome." A tall man older than Adrien approached us. Everything about him was heavy and thick—his stature, beard, and his glasses.

"Edmund, it's good to see you." Adrien clasped hands with the man.

My manners were forgotten in the sea of luscious fabrics. I found myself brushing my fingertips over each item, needing to feel their caress against my skin.

"What can I help you with today?"

"I need assistance building a wardrobe for my lady, Josselyn."

My focus returned when I heard my name. Embarrassed, I curtsied clumsily. "Well met, sir."

"None of that, little one," he laughed and clapped a giant hand on my shoulder. "It'll be my pleasure to dress you."

Without another word or question, he guided me into a smaller room at the back of the store. Fetching a small roll of tape from his pocket, he took my measurements in a midst of 'hmm's and 'ahh's. After scribbling a few hurried notes onto a small piece of paper, he disappeared and pulled a curtain over the entrance.

"Please undress while I'm out," he said through the curtain.

I undid the messy knots of my bodice and easily stepped out of the skirt, standing only in my underthings. It wasn't my first time being measured and fit for clothing. Jeremi and Victoria had taken me enough that the clothier in Anastas had my sizing memorized. I didn't wait long before Edmund returned with multiple options for me to try on, many of them for different occasions.

"This one I'll pack in secret." He winked and held up a white, lacy negligee that would leave little to the imagination.

I blushed furiously at the thought. I'd never worn a piece of clothing for someone else's entertainment—Victoria didn't see the point. I nodded, refusing to look into his eyes, and grabbed at the first outfit from the piles of clothing that lay before me.

For the next hour, I modeled clothing for Edmund and Adrien. With the ones I liked, Edmund would make adjustments with pins to the fit, and then take notes on his small pad of paper. He'd put the garment to the side to be tailored and delivered at a later time. Some of Edmund's choices I'm sure had Adrien's style in mind— one black dress was like nothing I had ever worn. It covered my shoulders and chest, but dipped in the back to a dangerous low, leaving my shoulder blades and lower back exposed. Both Adrien and Edmund's eyes widened as I drew the curtain. I pulled my long hair over one shoulder and turned to the side, revealing the dress's focal point.

"Perfect choice, Edmund. I knew I could trust your eye."

"You're a stunning girl, Josselyn." Edmund nodded his approval. "Only a few items left, yes?"

By the time I finished the stack Edmund imposed on me, I'd amassed traveling leathers, two elegant gowns for formal occasions, plenty of clothing to wear around Adrien's estate, and the negligee that he tucked away.

After everything we agreed on was marked and placed aside for adjustments and I donned new, more fitting attire for shopping in Valford, Edmund gave Adrien the total. My heart skipped a beat—I was accustomed to having things purchased for me but this was an extravagance I wasn't familiar with. Color rose to my cheeks as Adrien paid it without a second thought and shook Edmund's hand again with another smile.

"Thank you for your help, as always, Edmund."

"Of course, my lord. Come again, Josselyn, I'll be sure to put a few more things aside for you." He winked at me and I blushed.

"Thank you, Edmund," I said sheepishly. I took Adrien's free arm, assisting him in carrying the few items Edmund was able to quickly tailor from the store. "Thank *you, * Adrien."

"I told you, love, anything you desire." He shifted the parcels from my arms to his. "I'll return these to the carriage. Is there somewhere near here that interests you?"

I skimmed the shops surrounding us before my eyes fell onto a sign proudly displaying books. "Yes, that one."

"Ah, a reader are you?"

"Jeremi taught me. He was incredibly patient with me. I read everything I could get my hands on." I smiled.

"I see." He nodded. "Go on then, I'll catch up with you."

With newfound confidence, I crossed the threshold of the bookstore. Immediately, I was met with the scent of worn pages, leather bindings, and new ink. The Terryns kept a respectable library and the aroma reminded me of home. I breathed it in deeply.

The history of Rhoryn had always fascinated me. Possibly due to the amount of material Jeremi kept in his study. But my true love of stories lay in fairy tales. Stories of dragons, kings, and sorcerers with untold powers. Victoria would tell me a fairy tale every night when they first brought me to their home and I absorbed myself in them when I could read on my own. Sifting through the shelves and shelves of books I finally found a tome filled with them. I pulled it free and carefully thumbed through pages enchanted with intricate drawings and beautifully penned words.

"Excuse me, can I help you?" A man that could have been my grandfather stepped around the corner, peering at me through squinted eyes. "Elwyn's tits. A Whisper? Are you lost, girl?"

"N-no, I just—"

"You shouldn't touch things you can't afford." He deftly plucked the book from my hands. Anger warmed my blood.

"You don't understand—"

"Is there a problem here, Martin?"

"Ah, Lord Markov, just escorting this…lady to the door, you see."

"So you've met Josselyn, then?" Adrien kept his calm and took the book from Martin's hands. "Did you want to buy this, sweet? There may be another shop where we can find it with a more…congenial owner."

"I-I'm sorry, m'lord, I didn't realize she was yours—" Martin stammered.

"I am not anyone's to own," I snapped.

Adrien laid a hand on my shoulder. "Come, Josselyn, we'll search somewhere else."

"Just take the book, my lady. As an apology," Martin said, exasperated. "It's been years since I've run into one of you and times are tough."

"That's kind of you." Sarcasm dripped from Adrien's tone. He handed me the book. "Let's be off, then."

I hugged it to my chest, relishing in my small victory and trying to ignore Martin's harsh words.

"We still have four hours. What should we do next?" Adrien linked his arm through mine and continued leading me down the extravagant streets of Valford. I prayed for more acceptance and respect from its citizens. With Adrien by my side, I would have it.

V

We returned full and tipsy from the evening's remaining pleasures, laughing over trivial things. I held my book to my chest—my fiercely guarded treasure from the day. When we reached my bedroom, Adrien instructed one of the servant girls to unload the carriage into my wardrobe.

"There's one last thing I would like to give you today." He kissed the top of my head and took his leave while the servant carefully hung my new clothing. He returned after a short time with a rolled piece of parchment and a small box.

We both lay down on the bed as I unrolled the delicate scroll. My breath caught. I immediately recognized Jeremi's careful hand. I couldn't help but read the words in his voice, which brought an unexpected smile to my face.

Adrien,

I hope this finds you well and I apologize for the brevity of our last visit. I miss the days when we could lose hours in a tavern together, but my employer has kept me on a short chain this past year. Nevertheless, it's always wonderful to see you.

Victoria and I have finally asked Josselyn to become our Ring. Happily, she agreed. I wish I could have introduced you two, but in the light of recent events regarding the

Temple of Elwyn, I find myself wary of exposing her to the public eye.

To that end, if ill befalls me, I need you to promise me you'll seek out and take care of Victoria and Josselyn. I love them dearly and I fear the consequences if Elwyn's followers find them first. I'm sorry, but for now, this is all I can write. Send word if you visit Anastas again and I will make arrangements for the four of us to meet.

Best Regards,

Jeremi

We sat in silence for a time while I traced Jeremi's signature with my fingertips. My darling Jeremi. These were the last new words I would see from him. They resonated with my soul like a song. *Take care of Josselyn.*

"They both loved you deeply," Adrien said quietly.

"And I, them." They were gone and I was left without justice. An overwhelming desire to uncover the steps behind their murder rushed through my veins as I scanned his letter again. Something he'd written sparked another memory that had baffled me for some time. "What happened in the Temples that made them need to hide me?"

Around the time the letter was written, Victoria and Jeremi forbade me to leave the grounds without an attendant. They both made certain that I had all I needed within the estate, only making trips into the city when absolutely necessary. I missed our shared evenings exploring Anastas. However, I could never disobey them. Reading his letter brought a new light to the situation.

"The same year he wrote this letter, the followers of Elwyn began to forcefully oppose Rings. They denied Rings and their families access to the Temples and named them taboo. At the same time…Whispers were quietly disappearing without a trace. The faith never kept their silence on their opinions of your race. I believe it was too much for Jeremi and Victoria to risk."

"I see. Adrien…do you think the Elwyn followers were the ones who…the ones to…" I couldn't finish the sentence; it was too fresh in my mind.

"My dear, I do not know." Adrien took the parchment from my hands and rolled it neatly. "You may keep this if you like. But—" He handed me the small box— "yesterday morning, before I came to release you, I brought two members of my personal guard with me to salvage what was left of your belongings. Nearly everything was gone save for a few trinkets. However, this I thought you would want to keep close."

I removed the lid and inside was a ring of white gold that I instantly recognized as Victoria's. Its origin she had never explained, but she wore it always. It was a delicate thing encircled with tiny, precious stones. Inside the band, a jeweler from Lorelyn had engraved *Tere L'etai*—Love Freely—in Victoria's mother tongue. The creed of a Whisper. I slipped it over the tattoo on my left hand and admired it.

"It's…perfect. Thank you, Adrien. Truly."

Adrien's fingers brushed my cheek and he turned my face toward his own. "I will do anything for you. You need only say the words. Do you understand, Josselyn?"

"Yes." I felt a gentle tug at the corners of my lips. One last piece of each of my best friends—my soul mates—was more than I'd ever hoped for.

Adrien kissed my forehead, then my cheek, and then his lips traced the side of my face to the curve of my throat.

"It would be a tragedy to waste such a beautiful evening."

His fingertips trailed lightly along my skin; down my neck, past my chest, until finally alighting on my thigh. My body shivered in anticipation despite the warmth of the tavern's ale and his breath against my skin.

"All you need is ask," I murmured into his hair as I unhooked the clasp on his belt. "I am yours."

VI

drien's lips were silk against my skin. His lazy kisses down my spine raised gooseflesh with each careful inch taken. The bruises and bite marks on my shoulders and hips were just blossoming from the previous evening's pleasures. A smile tugged at the corners of my mouth despite the sting of my new marks. I stretched my bare legs, enjoying the sensation of the silk sheets caressing them. The sun hadn't yet shown its face through the grand windows of my bedroom, but Adrien's desire still ran hot.

"Well, good morning to you, too." I tried to laugh but my breath caught in my throat.

"Josselyn."

My name coming from him was like a song. After three months of his companionship, it still brought a familiar heat to my blood.

"Must you go?" he asked.

I sighed and turned to face him. His eyes were closed while the tips of his fingers caressed my inner thighs.

"If not today, my lord, when?" I muttered the question against his shoulder.

"Some…other day, perhaps?" As his hand moved my hips pushed themselves toward him. "I can think of better things we could do today."

"Adrien, it'll only be for one evening." I shifted myself to lie on the intricately embroidered pillows, pulling him with me.

He encircled me with strong arms and leaned in to whisper into my ear. "That is far too long, my sweet. I don't want to spend a single night without you."

I gasped as his fingers slipped inside of me. His eyes were open now; fire burned beneath silver.

"You may take me however you wish as soon as I return." My reply was strained as his deft hand worked me like a well-practiced instrument. I didn't want to leave him for a single moment; I wanted him close to me always.

"I *may* do that now." His teeth sank into my shoulder while his fingers ventured deeper, drawing moans I could not suppress. "You are mine, are you not?"

"I am—"

"My lady, your carriage is ready." A flat announcement came from the door.

One of the women in Adrien's employ had slipped through without either of us noticing.

Isabelle. From the moment I stepped foot into Adrien's home, she had reserved only the harshest of glances for me. She never spoke to me outside of common courtesy, and would only do what was asked of her, never going beyond minimum expectations. Adrien had given her strict instructions to treat me as she treated him, but her ire remained. It wasn't the first time she'd walked in on Adrien and me at an indecent moment and I had a feeling it wouldn't be the last.

"Damn you, Isabelle, all these years and you don't remember how to knock?" Adrien pulled his hand from me, leaving only an unfulfilled yearning between my legs. He shifted the sheets and left the bed, moving toward Isabelle without bothering to clothe himself.

Her emerald eyes concentrated on the floor, color rising to her cheeks. I would have bet my life that it wasn't embarrassment that hued her face.

"I'm sorry, my lord," she stammered. "I—"

"You seem to enjoy interrupting us more than any other steward in this household," he growled. "Why not join us?" It didn't sound like an invitation.

Without warning, Adrien grabbed a fistful of her auburn hair and forced the fingers that had only moments ago been inside of me into her mouth. Her eyes widened in surprise and a strangled noise tore from her throat. When she tried to pull away, he pushed his fingers in further.

"If you want to live in this place and continue spending my coin you will lick them clean." His voice was barely audible, but the threatening nature of his tone spoke volumes.

The look of contempt she gave me then would have struck daggers through any man.

But the desire that it evoked in me—her bitter gaze while she worked her tongue, Adrien's dominance over her, the wet sound of her mouth against his fingers, the thought of her sharing my bed…was something only a Whisper could feel.

"There's a good girl." His pleasure was obvious.

It took every ounce of restraint I had not to go to them and strip her down to mirror us. It seemed like so long since I'd felt the simultaneous touch of two people. I craved it like air. Adrien's actions with Isabelle were far more forceful than he dared do to me—and I hungered for him to treat me the same.

"If you've wanted my company so much, you should have said so. Josselyn is no stranger to the needs of women." Releasing her hair, he removed his fingers from her mouth.

Isabelle coughed violently before her enraged glare found its way back to me. "I would never lie with a wisp," she spat.

My blood ran cold, but the anger on Adrien's face made me fear more for Isabelle than I cared to admit. The strident crack of a hand connecting to flesh echoed throughout the room. Isabelle fell to her knees and cradled her face.

"You will never refer to Josselyn in such a way ever again. Do you understand me?"

"Yes, m'lord," she whispered. A tear raced down her cheek, but the slow-burning fury in her eyes told me it was not from physical pain.

"I didn't hear you." He took her hair in both hands and fiercely jerked her head to meet his piercing gaze. "Do you need more than just fingers to cleanse that mouth of yours?"

"Adrien, let her go," I interrupted. Every nerve of my body pleaded to let him do what he wanted with Isabelle, to let me join in. Yet, something in me said she didn't deserve it. "It's not the first time it's been said, nor will it be the last."

He turned to me in confusion. "She can't just call you—"

"It's alright. I think you've taught her as much."

The glance she spared me said she'd learned nothing from the encounter. Whatever angered her to such lengths…it didn't warrant this kind of punishment. Many years prior I had been in a similar position to Isabelle's and would have given anything for someone to champion me. I saw the same emotions cross her face that I'd carried then. Adrien released her hair.

"Get out of my sight." His words were sharp and cold. She would not be given another chance.

Isabelle scrambled from the room before he could say another word.

When she was gone, he sighed. "You shouldn't have interrupted me. She'll just—"

I shook my head and finally stood up to stretch, the aching in my joints both sharp and satisfying. I closed the gap between us before lacing my arms around his neck. "Don't throw her on the streets just because she's jealous. Maybe she'll come around."

He brushed the hair from my face and studied me carefully. "She must learn that she can't speak to you in such a way. If I don't stop that now—"

"She'll do what? Call me names until I cry? Adrien, you could employ this entire city if you wished it. She needs this job more than you need her. All of your other servants treat me like royalty, and her attitude is…refreshing."

His gaze softened. "You are a mysterious creature, Josselyn."

"Such is my nature." I smiled and kissed the curve of his neck. "She seems to fancy you. Have you two shared evenings together?"

"Many times." He moved from my arms to redress, not offering any other explanation.

The sudden cold disposition that took over him caught me off guard. Adrien wasn't willing to share much information about his past, no matter how much I pleaded. I may have let the conversation end if not for his immediate adverse reaction to my question. I crossed my arms over my chest and suddenly felt unsure of myself.

"Do you…Do you love her?"

He didn't turn to look at me, only continued picking up each garment from the floor. "It was not out of love that we shared a bed."

Not out of love? Out of habit? Necessity? "Then why—"

"Josselyn, it's not a matter that concerns you." His tone was final, and it pained me. After buckling his trousers he turned to me with an expression that said he was in no mood to discuss the matter. Besides, I had other plans that were already set into motion.

"I really must go if I want to arrive in good time," I said, watching him finish dressing.

He sighed deeply and took me in his arms. "Have a safe journey and I hope you find what you seek."

Another sudden shift in his mannerisms. I wondered what he was hiding from me. "As do I, love."

VII

Sitting quietly under Elwyn's peaceful gaze, I asked myself for the hundredth time that hour what force had brought me back to the Temple in Anastas. The very building that held me under lock and key—my life to be forfeit for a crime I did not commit. This was a place I never wanted to revisit, and yet, there I was. Elwyn's stare seemed to mock me—the vision of peace and harmony and the unknowing goddess to hundreds of ravenous wolves. I tossed a coin at her feet and bowed my head, wondering how one was supposed to pray. I repositioned my hooded cloak to cover most of my face and all of my hair.

My family sold me to slave traders before I could even grasp the concept of a religion. Once I learned of the many gods people worshiped, I felt no just higher power would ever allow me to suffer as I did. I decided to follow my own set of morals and pave my own life instead of counting on an unseen spirit.

Shortly after I became a member of the Terryn household, Jeremi explained to me why people felt the need to follow a force far superior to human existence—someone that would keep them safe from harm through prayer and faith. Victoria held her own religion that she practiced quietly, but Jeremi never believed in any sort of god or afterlife. I wondered if together they had crossed over into the peaceful sanctuary they both deserved. The vivid image of their lifeless bodies strewn across the bed crossed my mind again. The scene haunted my dreams and the scent of their blood was still fresh in my memory.

I was at the Temple because I had to know who killed the two people I loved most in this world. Afterlife or not, their deaths weighed heavily on my heart every single day. I needed closure desperately. I had no leads, evidence or proof. I didn't remember the faces or names of the guards that captured me that night or the people who kept me prisoner. Even so, the Temple was the first place they'd taken me immediately following the murders, and that was where I would begin my hunt.

Sweat beaded my brow and the insides of my palms. I did my best to keep my hands from shaking in fear. I couldn't go back to their dungeons. I wouldn't. I needed to stay strong.

"Have you come for Elwyn's blessing, m'lady?" The soft, deep voice of a cleric set my nerves on edge. I clutched the cloak tight around my neck and kept my eyes to the floor.

"No, Father, I have questions that beg answering." I glanced at my coin at the statue's feet. "But, if her blessing will answer them for me, then I'll gladly accept it."

Save for the cleric and me, the Temple was empty. It was the end of the working day when Elwyn's followers abandoned her in exchange for wine and carnal luxuries. The quiet hall was in my favor, however, as I needed to speak to the cleric alone.

"It's not often we have visitors at this hour."

My heart raced as his slippered feet approached in measured steps.

"Are you troubled, child?"

"More than you could ever know," I replied quietly.

"And to whom, if I may be so bold, do I owe these answers?" He took a seat beside me.

I did my best to look away from him, but a few strands of loose hair fell from their binding and outside the protection of my hood.

"A Whisper?" The warm words he'd shared only moments prior were immediately replaced by frigid tones and harsh emphasis. "Why are you here?"

"To know who killed my family, Father." I removed my hood and leveled my gaze with his.

The cleric was not what I had expected. Yellow hair framed a face that was all hard lines, set atop a thick neck and wide shoulders. Even covered by his robes of white and gold, it was obvious that he did not succumb to the extravagant lifestyles of many of the faith's leaders.

"Josselyn Thorn. You dare return here?" I didn't recognize his face from my stay in the dungeon, but my name came easily to his lips.

"The Terryns were a prominent name in Anastas. I'd hoped you could give me some kind of direction."

"They harbored no love for our prophet and were not ashamed to share their blasphemous opinions. Why should I help you?"

"Two people were murdered in their sleep in cold blood, does that not warrant any assistance? Is justice not something your gentle Elwyn seeks?"

His silence led me to believe the murder of two sacrilegious citizens—no matter how distinguished—wasn't any of his concern.

When he finally spoke, his words were deliberate and venomous. "While that may be true, I believe there was quite a bit of coin to be had from their deaths. Enough to entice their whore, perhaps?"

Rage tore through me and I struck him before I even became aware of the thought. He seized my wrist and gave it a sharp twist, eyes narrowing to slits.

"Get out." His tone was carefully measured. Pain jutted up to my shoulder. "I will not share words with Whispers or Rings."

I refused to give him the satisfaction of hurting me. How dare he address my family in such a way. "You have no idea—"

"I said get out!" he bellowed, throwing me to the ground.

I struggled to my feet before bolting to the door.

"I will throw you back in that cell if I ever see your face again!"

I ran as fast as my legs would carry me. Once again I found myself without direction or lead, too wary of the cleric's threat and too blinded by anger to consider my options. I wouldn't survive another day in their dungeons without a way to contact Adrien. My running turned a few curious heads but I paid them no mind. Once my breathing came in rasps, I slowed my pace to a brisk walk and collected my thoughts.

The Temple wouldn't answer my questions, the guards were a laughable consideration, and the few people that Jeremi and Victoria called friends would never have betrayed their trust in such a way. I needed to know who had alerted the authorities—city guards swarmed the scene not long after I found them dead. Without the cooperation of anyone involved, following that trail seemed impossible…

Before I realized where my feet carried me, I was standing before the Terryn estate. The place that I called home for so many years. Servants bustled in the gardens and I could hear voices echo from the main house. I remembered many lords and ladies who pined after the manor, and it seemed that one of them received their wish of ownership. I stood beneath the shade of an awning belonging to a long-standing apothecary nearby. The vines Victoria and I spent years growing blossomed beautifully against the white walls; I was happy to see them still there. A small pavilion to the left of the estate with pale lavender shingles where Jeremi spent countless, painstaking hours teaching me to read and write was still in pristine condition.

Other memories came flooding in and I took a moment to compose myself. I'd already shed more than enough tears; redemption was all I could hope for. But, my return to Anastas so far was fruitless, granting me only a ban from the Temple of Elwyn. There was one last person I hoped could give me any information at all and wouldn't fear what, or who, I was. I tore my eyes from the estate and made my way through the narrow streets of the crowded bazaar, ignoring the whispers and sidelong glances of curious citizens as I made my way to my destination.

The Cursed Elixir was an inn and tavern that began with a very small following five years prior to my Ring ceremony. Jeremi and Victoria both delighted in crowds, conversation, and excellent food. The Elixir prided themselves in all of that and more. Their rooms were some of the best in Anastas and even while living in a large estate, the three of us spent many an evening taking our pleasures there. Besides the superb company and drinks, the owner, Hilde Olrick, had always been one of the few people I felt confident in calling a friend.

Hilde was a large, joyous woman with a laugh that rang through every floor of her inn. Her jet-black hair was cropped short like a man's—to keep it out of the way of her work, she said—and her brown eyes were always smiling. On our first trip to the tavern, she never gave me the cautious glances I often received from other shop owners. She only remarked on how pretty I was and treated all of us like long lost family. She'd even offered us free samples of her food and spirits as well as delightful conversation. After that night, we made it a point to visit the Cursed Elixir at least once a week.

When I stepped through Hilde's doors, heard the quiet jingle of chimes as I entered, and saw her hustle between tables, it felt like home again.

"Welcome to the Cursed Elixir," she said as she carefully set a stack of plates into a wash basin. "Sit any—"

As her eyes moved to mine, the dishware fell into the basin with a loud crash. A few patrons looked her way but the regulars ignored it. She rushed toward me and swept me into her arms, hugging me tightly.

"Josselyn! Great gods, girl! After I'd heard about Jeremi and Victoria I thought you were…I thought—"

"I'm alive and well, Hilde. It's so wonderful to see you." It was hard to breathe under the pressure of her generous bosom. The comfort of her arms was a welcome reprieve. "Did a man named Sam come here earlier?" I asked that he meet me at the Cursed Elixir after I visited the Temple.

"Yes, but when he said your name I thought it couldn't possibly be you." She released me and fussed with the latch on my cloak, unhooking it. "But he insisted I tell you he'd return in the morning to take you home."

I sighed in relief. During our travels, Sam offhandedly mentioned he had family in Anastas and I was more than happy to suggest he visit them. An evening to myself was a welcome change.

"Is Sam your new sweetheart?" Hilde threw the cloak over her arm and eyed me suspiciously.

I laughed, wondering how clumsy, gentle Sam would ever handle me. "No, no Sam is just my driver. Jeremi's brother paid my prison bond. I've been living with him in Valford."

"Adrien? Now there's a face I haven't seen in ages."

"You know him?" I wondered how Hilde knew Adrien when I'd never heard a single word of him.

"He and Jeremi used to—"

"Hilde! The ale's dried up o'er here!" A bawdy patron interrupted us, raking his mug against the table twice before Hilde openly scowled at him.

"Loosen the strings on your corset, Robert, or you'll have nowhere to put that ale."

"Gods love ya, woman, ye got all night to chat. Just get us some more booze first!"

She ignored him and turned back to me. "Your favorite room is available. I'll put your cloak in there for you and we'll talk later. Pick any table you like, dear." She smiled apologetically before hurrying off, giving the man who interrupted us another reproachful glance. "Gods love *you*, Robert, you'd be wearing that ale if you didn't tip so damn well."

"You'll never find one as lovely as she. Treats you like gold, she does!" Robert's companion at the table laughed and toasted Hilde as she rushed away.

I smiled and took a seat at a table situated in a secluded corner. It allowed a clear view of the rest of the patrons with only half as much noise. Shortly after I situated myself, a large group of people entered the tavern. I realized my timing unfortunately aligned with her usual dinner rush. Hilde set to work, moving from table to table with a speed and accuracy that any swordsman would have admired. Alan, Hilde's husband, would be busy in the kitchen barking orders to a handful of apprentices to make sure food was served in a timely matter. The delicious smells of freshly cooked meats and baked goods wafted into the main hall. My mouth watered while I considered ordering a dish of my own.

As I predicted, Hilde's time for speaking with me was compromised for the evening. However, if she thought me dead, I had an inkling that any information of the murders had only come from the rumors of drunken patrons. Her knowledge of Adrien was what truly piqued my interest. I was sorting through the possibilities of how she met Lord Markov when finally she returned to my table laced with more apologies.

"Hilde, I'll have plenty of time to relive my tale soon. I'm just happy to be back here," I assured her and she shook her head.

"Let me at least get you something to eat."

"Does Alan still make his famous stew?" I ordered that stew more than anything else he ever cooked.

"Pretty sure there would be riots if he didn't."

"I'll take that then." I laughed.

"And to drink?"

"Whatever's in the house. Something red sounds perfect." Adrien didn't care for wine and I missed drinking it.

"Well, just this morning a case of some of the best wine in Rhoryn showed up. Fit for kings they say. I'll get you a bottle on the house, love."

"You've always been too kind to me. You don't have to do that."

"Nonsense, dear, consider it a homecoming gift. Back in a moment!"

Conversations of tournaments, politics, and the day's work overlapped each other, but the effect was relaxing. Normalcy after a mentally exhausting day of travel and reprimand. I thought back to my conversation with the cleric at the Temple and shuddered.

Though I should have expected them, his words cut me deeply. *I will not share words with Whispers or Rings*. Infertility was the obvious answer to their hatred—unnatural, they said—but I believed it was rooted much deeper than that. While Elwyn's followers only thought of us as prostitutes, it was said that Whispers held the ability to love more fiercely and openly than any normal person. Beyond our emotions, we harbored a very perverse physical skill set.

I suddenly thought of Isabelle and her cold glare as she sucked on Adrien's fingers. I thought of my hands twisted in her hair as she moved her mouth across my skin while Adrien explored me from behind. It had been so long since I'd felt the touch of two lovers and my body yearned for it more than I dared realize…

"Here we are, my lady." Hilde placed a goblet and plate in front of me; a welcome interruption to my thoughts. She gracefully poured the opaque red liquid into the glass until it filled a little more than halfway, and then set the bottle on the table. "The best year yet, they tell me. Worth a pretty coin. You came back at a good time."

"It's very much appreciated." I smiled and we both knew that I would tip graciously. I always did.

"You call me over if you need anything else, dear." She brushed my hair back affectionately and went to check on the other tables.

The wine was indeed delicious, and the numbing effect of the alcohol on my nerves was immediate. The stew was just as good as I remembered—the meat and vegetables cooked to perfection. Alan hadn't lost his touch.

I finished my food and near half the bottle of wine in good time. I was enjoying the quiet chatter of the surrounding patrons when I was approached.

"Well, well. What have we here? A wisp in Anastas?"

None of the patrons had given me more than a confused glimpse the entirety of the evening. Blood rose to my cheeks in anger. As I turned to confront the newcomer, my heart stopped.

His laughing eyes were like frozen water, his tousled, chin-length hair seemed to glow as snow does in moonlight, his skin was the color of caramel.

He was a Whisper.

VIII

"May I join you?" His smile was easy and brilliant. A slight, familiar accent not of Anastas or Valford touched his words.

I'd never met another like me. I didn't know what to say. "By all means." I motioned for him to sit and beckoned Hilde to bring me another glass. The moment it hit the table, I poured him a moderate amount of wine and passed it to him.

"Thank you…"

"Josselyn Thorn." I tipped my glass toward him before taking a sip. "And you are?"

"Cyprus Reyner. Well met." He took a hearty drink and looked at me curiously over his goblet. "Is there something on my face?"

I didn't realize I'd been staring. "I'm sorry, I've just never— I've never met…"

"Ah, yes, we are a rare species indeed. Tell me, Josselyn, do you think if two Whispers made love, time would stop?"

Maybe I should have taken offense, but the jest caught me off guard and served only to make me laugh. I couldn't remember the last time I'd sincerely laughed.

A few patrons at nearby tables gave us both wary glances, moving their chairs noticeably further away from us. Two Whispers in one place must have been quite the sight. They didn't know how to react and I didn't care.

"You are quite a forward thinker, my lord. But, I don't know. I've never tried." I drained my goblet and poured again until the wine was spent.

"I doubt any of us have." This time Cyprus waved Hilde to the table.

To her credit, she smiled at him as if he'd been there a hundred times. There was no contempt in her eyes like that of the other patrons.

"I'd like another of…whatever that is." He gestured casually toward the empty bottle.

"It's fairly expensive—"

Cyprus took a pouch from his side and set it on the table—the clear sound of coins clinking together could be heard over all other noise. Hilde smiled and bowed, leaving to fetch another bottle.

"Let's see, where should we begin?" Cyprus swirled his goblet in lazy circles, studying my face.

"Where are you from?" I asked. He hadn't recognized my name, which meant his stay in Anastas didn't extend beyond three months.

"A little place in the Isten Mountains. It's quite a ways out from here."

"Near Lorelyn?" My heart raced at the mention of Victoria's birth city. It explained his lilt—it was the exact inflection Victoria's words carried. I never had the opportunity to travel further than Anastas, even though I'd begged her to take me to visit her homeland on more than one occasion. The journey was long and arduous; she herself had only ventured it twice in my thirteen years of knowing her.

"*In* Lorelyn, actually. You've been there?" Cyprus raised an eyebrow.

"Not personally, but someone close to me was born there." I touched the familiar weight of Victoria's ring around my finger. His gaze moved from mine to my fidgeting hands.

"It's a beautiful place, especially when the snows fall on the Istens," he said slowly, focusing intently on my fingers.

A sudden sense of unease washed over me. I placed my hands in my lap self-consciously and continued our conversation. "And what brings you so far south of your home?"

His eyes met mine again and he sighed. "Work, unfortunately. Anastas is more in need of scribes than Lorelyn it seems. Delicate hands for delicate work."

He held up his left hand and wiggled his fingers playfully. He was right—his hands were slender and elegant, much softer and less calloused than my own. As I studied them, a small mark on one of his fingers caught my eye. I snatched his hand and examined it without thinking.

"Careful, my lady, this is my livelihood you're toying with."

"You're a Ring," I said, taken aback.

"I *was* a Ring." He pulled his hand from mine and his eyes said I'd pushed the limits of his comfort.

Hilde set the freshly opened bottle of wine onto the table with a sly glance in my direction before leaving us again.

Cyprus poured himself another generous glass and took a swig. "I haven't had enough wine for this conversation."

"Cyprus, so was I." I took a more gentle approach to my words. With help from my liquid courage, I revealed my hands again and shifted Victoria's ring to display my own intricate tattoo.

"Another Whisper that's also an ex-Ring. We seem to be quite the temporary luxuries." His laugh was dry—it was obvious that it was a story he wasn't prepared to tell. To be true, I wasn't sure if I was ready to tell mine, either. "But enough about me. You still haven't told me where you're from, lady Thorn."

"Anastas, actually. This is my home city. But...now I live in Valford." The wine was taking its toll, but the sensation was a pleasant one. It seemed as if every care I had only moments before had lost its urgency.

"That's a much smaller city. What made you move there?" Cyprus abandoned his search of my hands and searched my face as an artist studies a painting.

"Work." I laughed at my own joke, earning a confused smile from Cyprus. "It's truly a long story and too sad to retell over such good wine."

"Perhaps you'll be comfortable enough to tell me some day." The heat behind his gaze elicited a shiver that ran down my spine. The room wasn't as stable as I remembered it being only a few hours prior.

"I am curious, m'lord. I don't mean to bring up bad memories but, I...never considered a male Ring." Any Rings that Jeremi and Victoria spoke of were women—I had subconsciously come to accept that it was the norm.

"No? Have you never lain with two men?" His words were playful but something in his tone was serious.

"I...have never been offered the opportunity," I replied carefully.

"I suggest taking it if given the chance. I've only heard good things." He flashed a mischievous smile and split the rest of the bottle between our glasses, pouring mine first. He raised his glass and tipped it toward me.

"*Tere L'etai*," he declared.

"Love Freely," I responded without a thought, raising my glass in a mutual toast. It was engraved on the inside of Victoria's ring—I had memorized it long before Adrien gave it to me.

"You speak Reln?" His eyes widened in surprise.

"No, my...my friend from Lorelyn taught it to me." I didn't know the proper way to address Victoria to someone I just met. Even with his position as Ring, I wasn't ready to entrust him with my life story. Additionally, with the rumors of me as their murderess, I couldn't risk it.

He swirled his goblet in thought. I felt dizzy watching him. "It's such an interesting aphorism for our race, don't you think? But it opens a lot of doors, doesn't it?"

I thought of Adrien then, of his words to me that morning. *You are mine, are you not?* Was I, truly? Then why did I constantly feel as if something was missing?

"I suppose it does." I hardly felt myself lift my goblet anymore. The lights were hazy, the conversations muffled, my thoughts blurred. It had been ages since I'd consumed this much alcohol. "I am curious, though...if time would really stop."

What was I saying? I owed Adrien my life, my name. He'd saved me, offered me constant protection, and unlimited luxury. So why did it feel incomplete?

"Are you now?" He reached across the table and took my hand, brushing his thumb lightly across the top of my knuckles.

"This is...another opportunity I've never been offered." I heard the words but didn't recognize my own voice. Something in the furthest reaches of my thoughts told me to stop talking. To take my hand back. To return to my room and pretend these desires did not exist. But a greater force begged me to stay. I lifted the goblet to finish the last of my wine.

"Nor I." His cool lips against my skin set fire to my nerves. "Would you be so kind as to allow me to take advantage...?"

The liquid caught and burned in my throat. He laughed as I sputtered and coughed in response to his blatant statement.

"This situation, of course, is what I meant."

Forgive me, Adrien.

Before I could change my mind, I laid ten gold coins on the table. Plenty of money to pay for both bottles of wine, my room, and it would still leave Hilde a considerable tip. Cyprus left the small purse of coins he carried next to mine and shook his head when I tried to protest. Hilde would be more than pleased. I tugged at his hand while I stood. Leading us back to my room may have lasted seconds or years; it was impossible to tell as I stumbled through the upstairs hallway while Cyprus steadied me.

"A little too much wine, Josselyn?" His laugh was intoxicating. His mannerisms and voice set my heart alight and I could think of nothing more than wanting to feel those delicate hands caress every inch of me.

"Never too much wine," I giggled and drifted toward the wall before Cyprus caught me. The floor seemed to shift with every step.

We finally made it to the room and the door had scarcely closed before he pressed his body against mine, pushing me against the wall. He claimed my mouth with his, and his tongue eagerly parted my lips. Just his kiss took my breath away as his hands explored my curves. This wasn't the gentle foreplay I'd grown accustomed to—his desire was a completely different beast, and I hungered for it.

My hands wandered beneath the folds of his tunic. Immediately, he snatched my wrists and pushed them above my head, pinning them against the wall easily with one hand. His lips traveled from mouth to ear while his free hand invaded my top and teased my breasts. I cried out when I felt the sharp pinch of his fingers.

"I have a theory." His breath was hot in my ear and I shivered against his touch. "I think you like to have control. I want to see what happens when you don't."

His tongue traced the curve of my ear. Soft nips mingled with kisses while his hand worked relentlessly. Already I found myself gasping and covered in a thin sheen of sweat. I hadn't lost a single article of clothing.

"More," I begged as his mouth went from my ear to the curve of my neck.

His teeth sank deep into my skin and he sucked hard, his fingertips massaging, pinching, teasing.

My knees grew weak and I found it extremely difficult to continue standing.

Without warning, he stopped. He brought my hands down and all but threw me to the bed. The room spun violently. He removed his boots and began unhooking the laces from them.

"What are you doing?" I whined, my entire body throbbing in anticipation of his touch.

"Seeing as I've left my tools at home, we'll have to make do." The way he grinned as he said it made me desperately wonder what those tools were. Without further explanation, he pulled the ends of the leather cords away from his boots and approached me again.

He tore off my shoes, traveling leathers, and top, then ripped away my underthings without pause. I was completely exposed to him while he'd only lost his boots. He turned me on my stomach and forced my hands to meet behind my back. I felt the sudden kiss of leather against my wrists as he tied them together with his laces in multiple, complicated knots.

"So this isn't the first time you've done this?" I laughed and he replied with a sharp spank to my bare skin. I tensed and moaned.

"No, my lady, and I pray not the last." He massaged my hips and I felt his lips on my spine before his hand connected with me again. "If this is too much, please say something."

"We're Whispers. Is there such thing as too much?" I replied, breathless. I struggled against the bindings and found them tied incredibly well. My efforts received another strident slap against flesh.

"You won't be leaving anytime soon." He laughed under his breath and removed his tunic, casually ripping away a long section of fabric. "I never did like this shirt."

Rolling me onto my back, he straddled me at the hips. His chest was smooth and toned, set between strong, slender shoulders. Curved hip bones peaked above his trousers, framing a tight stomach. The need to taste his skin burned on my tongue.

He folded the cloth in thirds and placed it over my eyes, tying it securely behind my head "Can you see?"

"No, but the world is spinning."

"As it always has." Humor honeyed his tone.

Not being able to see him was frustrating. Not being able to touch him was infuriating. I'd never experienced the level of vulnerability that he brought me to in mere moments. He repositioned himself and without warning his lips were at my hip and his fingers were thrusting inside of me. I cried out and fought harder against my bonds.

"You will respond in kind to any pleasure given. Do you understand?"

"Yes," I gasped and pushed myself further onto his hand. His fingers knew every spot, every inch, every movement to bring me closer to climax.

"We're not done until I'm finished."

"As you wish, m'lord," I moaned.

His free hand spread my thighs wider and parted my folds. The hot, wet strokes that came next could only have been his tongue. My body responded to each stroke, my hips pushing harder against his mouth while his fingers continued to massage deep inside of me. His tongue explored every crease, teasing hardest at the points that made me cry out the loudest. My entire body trembled with pleasure. I wouldn't be able to hold back for long.

"I'm close," I whimpered. My words only encouraged him. In a few heartbeats' time, I climaxed, unable to suppress my cries. Instead of removing his hand, he only slowed his pace, his mouth moving to mine. He tasted like wine, cinnamon, and sex. His kiss was softer, fingers slower as he brought me down from the orgasm.

"Not tired yet, are you?"

"No." I smiled. "You know how we get."

He laughed and kissed me deeply again.

After exploring my mouth with his tongue for some time, his fingers left me and I could no longer feel his body pressed against mine. The sound of fabric hit the floor and he was on top of me again, but this time his bare skin caressed my own. He positioned himself on my chest above my breasts, seating himself at my collar bone.

"Now you'll be a good pet and return the favor." His hands twined themselves into my hair and he pulled my head up toward him, guiding my lips around his shaft.

The girth of him filled my mouth; he was already hard. I relaxed my throat and invited him in further with my tongue. His groans fed my desire as I worked. As much as I tried, I struggled to take the entire length of him.

"That's it," he breathed. His fingers tightened in my hair, pushing and pulling my head in the rhythm he desired.

My fingers ached to touch his skin, but every struggle against my bindings only served to tighten them. The primitive sounds that escaped him inspired me to slide my head further forward than I'd previously dared. The feeling of him hitting the back of my throat was enough for both of us to gasp for air.

"Just…like that." His words were split between his panting.

He pulled harder at my hair to quicken my pace, but I continued at my own speed. I could feel him throbbing. I knew every lap of my tongue brought him closer to climax. I dragged my tongue against every inch, forcing urgent cries from his throat. My name escaped his lips when the orgasm took him.

I swallowed every drop. The taste was sharp and distinctly his. It only fueled the fire that coursed through my veins.

He drew out of my mouth and lengthened his body on top of my own. The feeling of his naked skin touching mine was ecstasy. The darkness that swam before my eyes and unending vertigo were both new pieces of my reality. There was nothing else that mattered. His arms slipped behind me and he rolled onto his back, bringing me with him so I lay on top. He unbound my hands as quickly as he first tied them, then removed the blindfold from my eyes.

"Well hello there." I grinned and tried to steady the room. I leaned my forehead against his.

"Hello to you, my darling." One hand rested on the small of my back while his other hand cradled my face, thumb tracing the line of my cheek. "You have beautiful eyes."

"They're the same color as yours." My fingers danced across his skin, memorizing each line and curve. He felt even better than he looked.

"I beg to differ. Yours are like the sky just after it rains." He kissed each one of my eyelids.

"You're quite the charmer." I snuggled my head into the crook of his neck. "Does this mean you're done?"

"Quite the opposite, actually." His fingertips traced the long line of my back before squeezing my thighs. "I wanted to see your face."

He parted my legs and thrust himself into me before I could protest. My back arched and hips bore down on him in response. I felt so full. He was in so deep that with every gyration of my body, he massaged the back of me. Combined with his previous teasing, the sensations were overwhelming.

"Are you close already?" he mused. "You're so tight."

"Yes...I just..."

He took my hips in his hands and controlled his thrusts to a rhythm that promised I would not last long. Within minutes I was on the edge. As soon as the convulsions took hold, he pushed into me deeper and faster, dragging my climax out for as long as he could. I grasped at his arms, his shoulders, his hair, anything I could hold on to. His speed continued and my hips responded in kind. Finally, his cries joined my own as he climaxed with me.

We shared a few moments of silence—only the sound of our panting filled the room. I carefully moved to his side and our breathing slowed to an even pace. He wrapped his arms around me as I rested my head on his chest. His racing heartbeat matched my own and I smiled. Satisfaction took its hold and I found it incredibly difficult to keep my eyes open.

"Cyprus?"

"Yes, love?"

"Time absolutely stopped."

I closed my eyes and fell asleep in his arms to his soft laughter.

A series of loud knocks on the door that coincided with the pulsating throbs of my head woke me from a deep slumber.

"Lady Thorn? We must go if we want to make it to Valford before nightfall!" It was Sam.

The events of the previous evening flooded back and a whirlwind of emotions swept over me. I looked beside me to find my bed empty—Cyprus was gone.

"My lady?"

"I'll be right there, Sam." I massaged my temples. Why had Cyprus left without a word? On the pillow next to me lay a piece of parchment with beautiful handwriting and something tied to the bottom. The message was painfully short.

This belonged to someone that cared for you beyond her own life.

-C

I recognized the leather cord that had bound my wrists the evening prior; it now held a delicate necklace securely to the letter.

A large, amethyst-encrusted butterfly pendant hung from a simple chain. Victoria had always loved the butterflies in her garden…

I dressed as quickly as possible and gathered my few possessions that I'd taken for the journey. Hundreds of unanswered questions sped through my head. Two problems in particular burned at the forefront of my mind.

Who was Cyprus Reyner?

How in the seven hells was I going to face Adrien?

IX

The ride back was utter torture. The guilt that consumed me was unbearable as I fought with the options of telling Adrien the truth. The raw need that devoured me for Cyprus' touch was undeniable but completely inexcusable. Alcohol or no, I should not have given in. Adrien had done nothing but improve my well-being and I'd betrayed his trust. I felt ill.

One fact remained. Whether I liked it or not, I would need to find Cyprus again. Not only did he have information on Victoria, he knew her well enough to carry something personal of hers with him.

But, when I found Cyprus for the second time, would it only be to talk? The sensations of his hands on my hips, the leather biting into my skin, the weight of his body pressing into my chest—I feared I would not be able to stop myself from acting on my desires, even while sober.

The carriage came to a jarring halt, forcing me to double over and fall to the opposite seats. The dull throb in my head turned to pounding.

"Sam? Everything alright?" I called, wondering why the sudden stop.

"What're you hiding in there?" A voice I didn't recognize shouted.

Hoofbeats surrounded the cart and my heart stopped.

"Please, let us pass." I heard Sam's unwavering reply. For how shy Sam was, he certainly wasn't one to simply bare his throat in a dangerous situation.

The sound of boots striking dirt, followed by scuffling and frustrated cries, and then my door was thrown open.

"Seven hells, lads, we're rich." A rough, unshaved man with hair pulled away from his face grabbed my arm and forced me from my seat into the open.

"A wisp? Well, I'll be damned," one of the man's companions said, still on his horse.

"'Bout time we found something we can all share." The third bandit chuckled.

"Let her go!" Sam rushed the man holding onto me. He was pushed to the ground as easily as a predator bats away a flea.

"Please, sir, I'll give you whatever money you want," I begged, struggling to free myself from his grip.

"Oh, dear lady, you undervalue yourself." My captor sneered. His teeth were black and his breath was heavy with the scent of alcohol. "That dress alone is enough for another horse. Selling *you* would let us live comfortably for the rest of our lives."

"C'mon, Finn, don't hog her all to yourself."

"You're not taking her anywhere." Sam's voice held an unfamiliar tone.

Turning my head toward him, I realized he was attempting to confront Finn once more. This time with sword in shaking hand.

"Sam," I whispered, fearing for his life more than mine.

"You are a pesky little shit." Tossing me to the ground, Finn drew a sword from his side in one sure motion. "Your blood will be shed for nothing."

"I wouldn't do that if I were you." A new voice joined the fray.

A man with a square jaw and set shoulders held the third companion on his knees with a dagger to his throat. None of us heard him approach or unhorse the bandit.

"And who the fuck are you?" Finn's unwavering demeanor cracked at the edges.

"Just a hunter passing through. If the three of you wish to keep your precious hides, I suggest you ride west and warn the rest of your lot that this land isn't open for heists."

"The Thicket don't belong to no one—"

Finn lost his opportunity to retort when the hunter slit the throat of the man he held without the slightest flinch.

"Elwyn's tits man, calm down." Finn dropped his sword.

I crawled back toward the carriage, taking Finn's sword with me. I did my best to mask the tears that hid behind my eyes. Sam rushed to my side.

"You bastards stay away from here, do you understand?" Our savior tossed the lifeless body aside and sheathed his dagger, only to pull a sword from his hip.

"Fine, keep the stupid twat." Finn spat in my direction before mounting his horse. He looked at his remaining companion and jerked his head.

"But, Nick—" His companion stared at the blood pooling on the dead man's shirt.

"A'int nothing for him now, brother. Let's go."

We watched them gallop away until they disappeared behind the trees.

Sam clasped my shaking hands in his. "Are you alright?" All color was drained from his face—it looked like he'd seen a ghost.

All I could offer him was a nod.

"My lady, forgive me for the violence. I'm Isaac." He sheathed his sword and stepped over his kill as if it were a trifling obstacle. He turned to Sam. "Son, I don't know if that was the bravest or dumbest thing I've ever seen."

"It's Sam." Sam grasped hands with Isaac, ignoring his comment. "What brings a hunter so far south?"

"A herd of elk I've been following moved this way. You're lucky they did, else you'd be skewered on the edge of that sword." Isaac motioned toward the blade in my hands.

"I don't know how to thank you, Isaac," I murmured. My headache I'd all but forgotten returned and the incessant pounding was amplified tenfold. I wanted nothing more than a hot bath and a meal.

"And I don't know what possessed you to travel alone. At least bring a bodyguard, lady…"

"Thorn. Josselyn Thorn," I supplied.

"Well, Lady Thorn. At least allow me to escort you back to Valford. Though, I have no doubt your driver is quite fierce." Isaac glanced at Sam. Color returned to his pallid cheeks.

"Sam saved my life," I countered. If it weren't for his bravery, I was sure Finn wouldn't have spared a moment riding off with me. I caught the smile that pulled at the corners of Sam's lips and felt better. He didn't deserve the ridicule.

"That he did, my lady. Now, give me a moment to take care of our silent friend here, and we'll be off."

Isaac shouldered the bandit's body like a sack of flour and disappeared into the forest.

"Sam, thank you." I squeezed his hand and settled myself back into the cart.

"Of course, Lady Thorn." Sam bowed and closed the door, making his way toward the horses.

"Well, shall we go?" Isaac reappeared moments later, brushing his hands against his pants. Seating himself on his horse's saddle, he led us back toward Adrien's estate.

Despite the ambush in the Verdant Thicket, the rest of our journey felt painfully short. I found myself at the estate before I was ready to look Adrien in the eye. Sam opened the door for me when we reached the courtyard, but Isaac was quick to move to my side and offer me his arm. I met his gaze and moved past him. The smirk he wore said he expected it, but I hoped it still wounded his pride.

Adrien was sitting in the hall with a book in his hands. When his gaze landed on the three of us, he was on his feet.

"Josselyn, are you all right?" His eyes shifted from me to Isaac and back. He took my hands in his and studied my face.

"I'm safe, m'lord. Thanks to Sam and Isaac." I nodded, unable to meet his gaze.

"Isaac?" Adrien asked, turning toward the hunter.

"A hunter, my lord. These two were stopped by bandits not far from my camp. But those men won't be a problem in the Thicket any longer," Isaac explained, crossing his arms.

"Isaac, Sam, stay here with me a few moments if you would." Adrien turned to me, brushing my face with his fingertips. "Go get cleaned up. We'll talk later. You're safe now, sweet."

I nodded once more and made my way to my quarters. To my surprise, it was Isabelle who greeted me in the hallway. Her eyes were lowered, but I knew the contempt she bore was still there.

"Adrien instructed me to bathe you personally upon your return, my lady. To atone for my...*misgivings*." She didn't bother hiding her resentment.

I couldn't blame her for it. I was curious as to why he commanded her to do so, though. I didn't think he would trust her alone with me after the previous morning.

"Thank you, Isabelle," I replied.

Her eyes pierced me then. "I don't want your pity, Whisper."

I bowed my head and she turned with neither a word nor gesture to follow her. I ignored her angry disposition—I was too tired and too preoccupied with my own worries to let Isabelle's words bother me. I trailed behind her, maintaining a fair distance between us. Her long red locks were tied into a bun at the base of her slender neck. I very much wanted to unbind it and coil my fingers through the curls. The fury she held for me without reprieve made me want to force it out of her screaming. Despite every uneasy feeling knotting in the pit of my stomach, everything about Isabelle drew me to her like a moth to flame. The subtle aroma of her perfume, her elegant eyelashes, the set pout of her lips, the way her body swayed as she walked…

I rubbed my still-pounding head to clear the thoughts as we entered my chambers. She'd already prepared a scalding bath scented with various perfumes and oils. I undressed, daring not ask her for help, and stepped gingerly into the water. She went to work immediately, running her fingers through my hair to break the few tangles that had formed in the day's journey. Tipping my head back, she methodically ran water through the strands. The familiar smell of soap wafted through the room and her fingers set to scrubbing my scalp. The room was silent beyond the occasional splash of water and every twist of discomfort in my stomach tightened. I wished I could say something to her to make her feel better. To make her not hate me so much.

"Isabelle…what have I done to upset you?" I chanced.

She was silent for a long time, her focus set on washing my hair. I began to wonder if she would ignore me for the duration of the bath. Without warning, she clutched two fistfuls of my hair and yanked my head back. I gasped…but not out of pain.

"What have you done? What *haven't* you done," she snarled.

"Wait—" I moved my hands on top of hers and her grip tightened.

"You have a place in this house and food in your mouth without needing to lift a single finger—"

"That's not…entirely true."

I whimpered when she pulled my head back further, exposing my throat. She leaned her body over me so her eyes met mine.

"You asked me a question. Spare me your sarcasm." Her furious tone sent a chill over my entire body despite the hot water. "Stop looking at me like that!"

"Like what?"

"Like I'm your next meal," she snapped. "All your kind thinks about is sex. No matter the circumstances, if you've set your sights on someone, you won't give up until you take them."

"Forgive me. I just—"

"Shut up!" She shoved my head forward and released my hair. My scalp throbbed from the pressure of her fingernails. "I saw how you looked at me yesterday when Adrien…when he made me…" Isabelle's voice faltered. Her hands went to the cheek Adrien struck. "I wish you would've died with the rest of your disgusting family."

"Isabelle! That's enough!" Adrien bellowed from the door.

I started and turned to see his handsome face corrupted in fury. I tried to swallow the lump that had formed in my throat from Isabelle's poisonous comment. Adrien's anger terrified me. If he noticed how her words affected me…I didn't want to consider what he was capable of.

"Fine." Isabelle moved from beside the bath to the door where he stood. She raised her gaze to his, meeting it without flinching. "She's your toy. You wash her."

When Adrien raised a hand against her, Isabelle caught him by the wrist in an impressive show of speed.

"You don't have to force me *out of your employ.* I'll see myself out." She took her leave without another word.

"Josselyn, are you alright?" Concern blurred with the fury in his eyes. I stood from the tub and reached for the nearby towel, steadying my shaking hand.

"I...Adrien, don't let her leave like this." I fought the tears that burned the back of my eyes. *I wish you would've died.* Part of me wanted to let him serve whatever repercussions he had in mind to his rebellious servant. Even so, the gentleness Isabelle's features took when she spoke of Adrien, the terrible things she said about Whispers—Isabelle's demons were at work and it pained me that I couldn't be the one to quell them. "Please, just talk to her."

His eyes drifted the length of my body. I knew he had other ideas having nothing to do with helping Isabelle. "Does she really deserve any kindness after that?"

"She needs you. Adrien, please."

Adrien closed the gap between us and kissed my forehead, slowly running a hand through my hair. "Get dressed and find something to eat. We'll speak of your trip to Anastas later."

I nodded and he turned to leave. In mere moments, I stood alone in my chambers staring at the closed door. I sank to my knees and silently wept into the lush towel.

X

ours passed. The moon showed its full face through the many windows in the estate as I wandered the hallways. I'd long since dressed and fixed something to eat, with Lily fussing over my every move. Adrien still hadn't come to find me. I wondered how Isabelle was, if he took my words to heart, or…

I shivered.

I came to a door that displayed Adrien's name carefully engraved into a plaque. On our short tours of the estate, he told me that it was his study, but mentioned that it wasn't worth notice. Curiosity got the best of me and I tried the handle, finding it unlocked. Adrien never talked to me about his work. He said it wasn't something that concerned me so long as it supported me.

Carefully easing the door open, I found the room only lit by moonlight. A lamp hung from the wall by the door and I reached in to twist the bottom mechanism. The entire room was soon illuminated in a warm yellow glow. I slipped through the door and closed it behind me.

The office was one of the smaller nooks in the estate, containing one well-organized bookcase, a desk, and two chairs. I went to his desk and found various feathered quills lined beside an ink pot. The mahogany gleamed with fresh polish and every item on the surface had its own home. Sitting in his fine leather chair felt luxurious and I could imagine myself falling asleep in it with ease. Following the smooth material with my fingertips, I found the desk contained three drawers. As I glanced over them, a gleam from one caught my eye. A lock dangled from the handle, but it was unfastened. Despite my best judgment, I moved the lock and opened the drawer to find a thick stack of official looking papers bound by a cord. My heart raced as I removed the bundle and placed them on the table.

The document on top began with a carefully penned header from the Temple of Elwyn. I scanned through the small writing, realizing it was the terms of my release. My name and Adrien's were mentioned multiple times, followed by the amount due for my freedom. My heart skipped at what it cost Adrien to take me away from that dungeon. He could've purchased Edmund's entire clothing line and still had enough to feed every servant for a week. At the bottom were Adrien's and Father Bastion Rochefort's signatures. Father Rochefort served as the head of the Temple of Anastas for as long as I could remember. I thumbed through the papers, careful not to leave so much as a crease. Work contracts for each of his servants, the deed to his Estate, bank ledgers, shipping manifests, nothing of interest to me…until the final page.

OFFICIAL NOTICE OF SALE

Compensated Parties: Gillian and Jacquetta Thorn
Included item(s): Josselyn Thorn
Description: Female, twelve years of age, appears to be in good health. White hair, blue eyes, light brown skin—more commonly known as a "Whisper."
Amount to be paid: 1,000 Gold Coins
Purchasing Parties: Bastion Rochefort

The document was dated accordingly and signed by every party. I don't know how many times I re-read each word.

Confusion, rage, despair, anger, and other emotions I couldn't name twisted in my heart. It was the same man that signed me over to Adrien, allowing me my freedom. Why would he do such a thing thirteen years later if he purchased me in the first place? It didn't make sense. Scribbled in an impatient hand, the bottom left corner read: *"To be auctioned at the City of Ends."*

My parents sold me for a mere thousand gold, and Father Rochefort put me in the stocks at the City of Ends to turn more of a profit. I forced myself to put the papers back in the drawer exactly as they were before closing it. It took every ounce of my willpower to not scream and tear the document to shreds. Why did Adrien have my notice of sale? Asking him was impossible. He couldn't find out that I was sifting through his things.

I stood, pushing the chair back to where I found it. I took the few long steps to the door where I cut the fuel to the lamp. If time passed it was unclear. The moonlight still illuminated the long hallway as I closed the door behind me.

My mind ran in circles as I made my way back to my room. What would I do? How dare my parents give me up so easily. Were they told of the auctions? Did they know what hell they put me through? Did they care?

Muffled voices behind a door halted my steps. Dim lamp light peeked through a crack barely wide enough for me to see through. Articles of clothing were strewn about the floor in a line toward the large bed. Red curls spilled down an arched, porcelain back. Red silken sheets barely covered the gentle curves of her backside. Hands encouraged her hips to move in a slow, steady rhythm as sighs escaped her throat.

"I need you, Isabelle." Adrien's voice was unmistakable although I couldn't see him from my vantage point.

My entire body froze.

"I know." She laughed under her breath. "You're terrible at showing it."

"*You* could stand to be nicer," he replied.

She leaned over him, creating a supple, sensual line with her back.

Adrien's moan drifted above her sighs. "That's a good way to start."

"I love you, Adrien," she whispered.

"I know," he replied.

I backed away from the door and hurried to my chambers. I felt empty and used. Isabelle was right. I was nothing more than Adrien's toy. A commodity. I asked Adrien to spare his fury for nothing. He never planned to let her go in the first place.

I had to get back to Anastas, to Cyprus. I had to find Bastion Rochefort and glean any inside information on the auctions and his connection with Adrien.

I slammed the door to my room and locked it. Adrien could wait until morning to speak with me if he so pleased.

I found the negligee Edmund slipped into my clothing purchases what felt like ages ago and tore it to shreds with my bare hands. Stoking a fire in the large hearth, I sat before it and watched every piece of the thin fabric burn to ash. I never had the chance to wear it, and for that, I was grateful.

Adrien Markov didn't deserve me.

XI

I had to escape Adrien's estate. There were so many questions that remained unanswered in both Valford as well as Anastas, but I would never find them under Adrien's careful supervision.

Despite my overwhelming exhaustion, sleep evaded me that night. I kept the fire stoked and thumbed through my book of fairy tales. Each story of fearsome dragons, valiant knights, and powerful magic was read to me in Victoria's gentle voice. They eased my aching chest and brought substance to the holes filling my heart. The sun shined through my window when there was a knock on my door.

"Josselyn, may I come in?" Adrien's satin voice carried easily to my ears.

Images of the previous evening played through my head in perfect clarity. The trail of clothing strewn across the floor. Isabelle's naked back toward me, her hips moving with Adrien's, his hands on her sides. *I need you, Isabelle.* Feelings I managed to stifle with my book of stories returned, pulling the air from my lungs. My emotions were torn to shreds. I felt awful for my anger with Adrien—his act of betrayal was a mirror to my own with Cyprus. However, Adrien had assured me there was nothing between him and Isabelle. Catching them in bed together…it painted a different picture.

Adrien jostled the door handle but the lock held firm.

"Josselyn?"

"Leave me alone," I mumbled. I felt pathetic. If Adrien knew what I had done, would he feel the same way? Did he see his actions as a betrayal?

"What's the matter, sweet?" There was a pause and I didn't answer. "Please let me in?"

It seemed I wouldn't rid of him with just my silence. I stood and stretched my aching joints from sitting in the same position for so long. I took my time approaching the door. When my hand touched the cool metal of the handle, I exhaled and closed my eyes in an effort to calm myself. I opened the door and Adrien stood before me, the very image of patience and understanding. His handsome face was contorted with worry and his silver eyes gleamed with genuine concern. There was nothing about his demeanor that said he had something to hide. He reached toward me for an embrace and I flinched. Concern turned to confusion.

"Where were you all night?" My voice shook—I couldn't help myself.

"I took your words to heart. Isabelle did need me to talk with her," he replied. His tone was soft as if any aggression at all would break me.

"*Talk*," I spat. I wanted to grab his shoulders and shake the truth from him.

His gaze fixed on my own and he reached for me once more. I took a step back.

"I saw you two together," I said, accusation dripping from every word. "You have a fascinating means of talking to someone."

"Isn't your creed 'Love Freely?'" he questioned. "I would think if anyone understood sharing your desires with another, it's you."

Love Freely, not Use Freely. I thought, bitterly. "Are you saying you love her?"

"Josselyn, I told you when you first came here, she means nothing to me." He stepped into the room and closed the door behind him.

"Then why do you *need* her?" I could taste the venom in my reply. "She loves you, Adrien. And from what I've seen, I think she means far more to you than 'nothing.'"

"Would you have cared as much if I invited you to bed with us?"

"You're avoiding my question."

He sighed and shook his head. "Isabelle's family and mine have worked together for generations. Isabelle's not just a servant here, Josselyn. She helps me with accounting, bookkeeping and managing all of the other servants. Sometimes she makes trips for business in my stead. If I lose her, not only do I gain the ire of her family, I'm losing out on an associate."

I never considered Isabelle to be more than a servant to Adrien. It was clear she harbored a sharp wit, but I hadn't realized how much she actually did for him. Despite his explanation, my unease remained.

"Why didn't you just tell me?" I demanded.

"I couldn't risk severing ties with her and her family because you two hate each other. From every standpoint, it doesn't make sense."

"I understand but...did that require taking her to bed without consulting me?" My resolve was faltering and he could see it.

This time on his approach, I didn't back away. He pulled me into his arms and held me close, his heartbeat steady and calming.

"No one could ever replace what you are to me." He stroked a hand through my hair.

"And what is that?" I murmured into his chest.

"Everything I've ever wanted *and* needed." He kissed the top of my head. "Josselyn, I love you."

My breath caught and my thoughts froze. The words he spoke sounded sincere. His tone reminded me so much of Jeremi. Still, in a true search of my heart, I couldn't give him the answer he sought.

"I understand if you don't trust me." He put one hand beneath my chin and tipped my head up to meet his gaze. "At least let me show you."

Adrien's lips met mine in the softest kiss he ever bestowed on me. I closed my eyes and melted into it, circling my arms around his neck and pulling him into me. In all of our encounters he was gentle, but this was the first display of tenderness. His hands moved to the small of my back as his tongue teased my bottom lip. My frustrations dissolved with every shared breath despite my efforts to cling to them. He pulled away to lift me into his arms and carry me to the bed. I wanted to tell him to stop. That the scenes tainting my desire were still playing through my head. My body yearned for him while my heart held mistrust.

A handful of seconds passed before he lay me down and positioned himself over me, caressing my mouth with another long, affectionate kiss.

My hands wandered with their own intentions, crawling beneath his tunic and tracing the muscles of his chest. His lips moved from my mouth to graze the long line of my throat, drawing sighs from mine.

"Adrien—" I whimpered.

"It's alright, love," he whispered against my skin. "Just enjoy yourself."

He moved to loosen the strings of my nightgown, his hot breath close behind his fingers. The touch of his lips set my nerves singing. After baring my chest, his hands continued south but his mouth lingered near my breasts. My back arched in anticipation and he answered with his tongue. Fire raced through my veins, setting my body aflame. Every touch, every kiss, every caress; Adrien exploited each point of pleasure he had gleaned in our time together. His fingers reached their destination and eased inside, filling me until I moaned in satisfaction.

For the first time in my life, I felt betrayed by my own body. Adrien didn't give me a chance to consider his words, to find comfort with his relationship with Isabelle. I thought of Cyprus asking me if what he was doing was too much. Adrien never offered me a similar opportunity. I thought of Jeremi and Victoria, who continuously asked how I was feeling in place of their own comforts.

Despite all of these memories, I found my hands unhooking his belt and trousers with practiced dexterity. I needed to feel him inside of me. I needed release. My whole being shook with it. My blood screamed for it.

"Always so eager." I could hear the smile in his voice. "You'll always have what you want, Josselyn."

What do I want?

Adrien's mouth covered mine as he replaced his fingers with himself. I gasped, gripping his shoulders while he set a slow, deliberate pace. My hips matched his rhythm and I kissed him hungrily.

I wanted to feel like I had any emotional stake in what was happening. I wanted to have control over my carnal desires. I wanted someone to love me for who I was, not what I was.

I shuddered, waves of ecstasy washing over me each time Adrien thrust into me. My body tightened and clenched. His pace quickened—he was close. His low moans blended with mine. My fingernails dug into his skin.

I wanted Cyprus.

"Come for me," he urged.

And I did, as he knew I would.

I cried out, wrapping my legs tightly around him. He plunged deep into me as he climaxed, drawing rasped breaths against my lips. I trembled in satisfaction and he kissed me once more before lying beside me and pulling me close. Our breathing slowed and before words could be exchanged, he fell asleep. I turned onto my side, repositioning myself against him.

In case he woke up, I didn't want him to see me crying.

XII

I hadn't experienced such vivid, violent nightmares in months. Memories that I worked so hard to suppress rushed back to me in excruciating detail. Visions of thirteen years prior; a giant, ugly man handing my parents a bag of gold. He stared at me like a prized horse while my family avoided any final contact with their child.

I remembered the sensation of his soft, leather gloves gripping my bare skin with perfect clarity. I begged and pleaded for my mother to change her mind as he threw me into the carriage without remorse. I was their daughter. How could they hand me over in exchange for a few pieces of metal?

I was taken to a cold, dimly lit basement where others my age and older—both male and female—were chained against the walls. In the center of the room loomed an instrument I would grow to hate.

"'Don't hurt the wisp,' eh?" the man muttered.

He tore away what was left of my clothing, leaving me exposed to the hollowed eyes of every other person in the room. Out of all of them, I was the only Whisper.

They'd reserved the pillory for me.

"I'll watch where I bruise, then." His sardonic tone set me to shivering.

In one swift movement, he opened the top of the device, forced me down onto it, and locked me in. Leather gloves caressed my inner thigh as a fresh stream of tears cascaded down my cheeks onto the stone floor.

"Please, no—"

"You're purchased property now, wisp. Your mummy and daddy gave you up." I heard him unfasten his trousers and my entire body clenched in response. "'Sides, I heard some interestin' things about your kind…"

The look of horror on the others' faces only made it worse. They would watch, and they could do nothing.

"Don't. Please don't," I whimpered to deaf ears.

But he did. And so did every other man in his employ. Perhaps not the same day, but seven guards in total had their way with me dozens of times in that room for the longest eleven days of my existence. If I fought too fiercely, they'd strike their crops across my back.

Don't hurt me, they were instructed. It had fallen on deaf ears.

I was still so young. I had never known the touch of a man— barely old enough to even give it a thought. They didn't care. They were ruthless.

"Stop!" I shot awake, sweat coating my skin and the sheets surrounding me. Tears streamed down my face and I could barely make out the form before me. When my vision cleared, I was surprised to see a stunned Isabelle standing above me. Her hand hovered in the air as if she was considering reaching out to me.

"Josselyn—" She dropped her hand to her side, but her eyes remained wide— "You…were screaming in your sleep…"

I rubbed my eyes and pushed the hair from my face. Adrien was no longer by my side. I took three rasping breaths before daring to speak. "What can I do for you, Isabelle?"

"Adrie—Lord Markov…wants to see you in the dining hall," she reported, careful not to address Adrien so casually.

"Thank you." When I looked at her, I couldn't help but notice the new pair of earrings that dangled from her ears. They were clearly precious stones. My stare must have fixed for too long because she moved to self-consciously toy with one earring.

"I'll take my leave." The curt Isabelle I knew resurfaced. As she turned, I caught her wrist. Her eyes flashed to my fingers, but she didn't pull away.

"Isabelle, listen to me," I pleaded. "I don't truly understand why, but…Adrien is using you for his own gain. You need to be careful."

She studied my face for a long time. "Why would you tell me this?"

I dropped her hand and repositioned the sheets so they covered my naked body. "Because you deserve better than him."

"Are you trying to chase me off?" She crossed her arms over her chest. Her eyes narrowed. "Do you want me gone so he may see you as more than a plaything?"

"He sees us both as playthings," I muttered, toying with a loose seam on the edge of a pillow.

"You don't know him like I do, Josselyn. I've stood by his side for years. He holds me in a far higher regard."

"Maybe you're right. Maybe he just tells me differently," I replied bitterly. "I just don't want to see you hurt."

"Why do you insist on constantly playing my hero?"

She never spared me a friendly word, yet that was all I offered her. I wondered if it only served to anger her further. "I know what it is to be used and manipulated while others look on. You're a beautiful, intelligent, young woman and you deserve more kindness than Lord Markov affords you."

"And you're a manipulative, lust-driven wisp," she snarled. "Who wants nothing more than to take everything from me."

I was too exhausted and emotionally drained to give her words any credence. If she was adamant on remaining by his side, there was nothing I could do. "Perhaps one day you'll give me the chance to change your mind."

Isabelle barked an incredulous laugh and took her leave.

Despite her sour mood and hurtful words, she hadn't been able to hide everything from me. I'd seen the concern that wracked her features when I woke from my nightmare, her acceptance of my touch, and the creeping doubt edging itself into her gaze when I warned her of Adrien. Isabelle was no fool, she would think on what I said regardless of her demeanor.

I dressed and made my way into the dining hall where Adrien awaited me, nursing a glass of brandy. Only then did I realize how late I must have slept. I joined him, picking a few grapes from a nearby fruit bowl.

"I'm glad to see you among the living." He smiled easily. I had trouble meeting his eyes—my heart was still in contention with my body.

I nodded. "I hadn't slept the previous night. I fear I've wasted our day."

"We'll have other days, sweet." He took a sip of his drink. "I needed to tell you, I've been summoned for work in Veritas. It's a few days' ride from here and I'll be gone for nearly a fortnight. I've left Isabelle in charge of managing the estate. Bearing her…aggressions…in mind, are you comfortable staying here? I could find you another place to stay—"

"I appreciate your concern, but I'll be fine on my own." Adrien leaving was my chance to escape the estate and search for Cyprus. Bandits or no, I couldn't waste such an opportunity. Relief humored my words. "Will *you* be alright on your own?"

"I did consider taking you with me. It's going to be very lonely without you." He reached across the table for my hand.

I entwined my fingers with his and remained silent.

"With the bandit attack on your last journey, however, I'm loath to risk it."

"That's kind of you." I smiled. I wondered what the real reason was. "You'll be safe, won't you?"

"The time will pass before you know it." He kissed the top of my hand.

I wanted to pull away but refrained.

"There's one thing I must ask of you," he remarked.

"What's that?"

"Please, for the sake of your safety and my sanity, don't travel anywhere without me. When I return, we'll go anywhere you wish. I don't know what I'd do without you."

Find a new toy to play with, I thought bitterly. "You have my word."

"Thank you, Josselyn." He sighed in relief.

"When do you leave?"

"In the morning at first light, I'm afraid. I wish I had more notice. I just couldn't pass up such a good opportunity."

When I'd previously asked Adrien about his work, he explained to me that the finer details were extraordinarily complicated. Essentially, he imported expensive goods from one city to the next throughout Rhoryn so they may be in the hands of nobles faster than any courier. During my time with him, he received only one other summons and he was gone for a handful of days.

"Why don't we go to the tavern and enjoy your last night here, then?" I needed the fresh air. And gods knew I needed the wine.

"That sounds like a wonderful idea." He tipped his glass toward me. "Let's be off."

XIII

The estate was still bustling with energy despite Adrien's absence. Isabelle managed the servants easily and daily life continued without a hitch. Without Lord Markov to keep watch of my every move, I began to pack a bag of necessities for my travels to Anastas. I was terrified to make the trip alone. No matter how many weapons I armed myself with; I was no match against sheer numbers. However, going by myself I saw as a necessity to prevent word from getting to Adrien. He seemed to have the undying loyalty of every person in his servitude and I trusted he would know within a day's time.

I finished preparations two days following his departure, hiding my belongings beneath my bed to not raise suspicions as the servants came and went. I pondered what to do with my final time in the estate. With nothing left to lose, I took a gamble.

As I knocked on the door to her chambers, I reconsidered how clever my idea really was.

"Who is it?" Isabelle's voice drifted through the thick oak.

"It's…Josselyn," I replied.

There was a long silence. I was about to give up on my idea when her voice answered. "Come in."

I pulled the latch and pushed the door open. Isabelle lounged on a line of pillows, leisurely reading in front of the fireplace. It was the first time I ever witnessed Isabelle at rest in the estate. She was constantly moving around—ensuring every aspect of the manor was perfect. I was glad she took some time to herself.

"What do you want?" She didn't bother looking up from her book.

"Adrien left me a large sum of money to use as I wish." I smirked. "And…I wish for you to accompany me into the city tonight."

Isabelle turned a page of her book. "Why?"

"So we can reintroduce ourselves." She looked at me then. "Or, I can buy you another expensive pair of earrings."

Color hued her cheeks. She sighed. "Fine. When?"

"As soon as you're ready, my lady." I smiled, relieved.

"Go back to your room. I'll fetch you when I'm done." Isabelle closed her book.

For the first time in days, my heart felt lighter and my spirits lifted. I didn't care why Isabelle accepted my offer—just that she had. Once I departed Valford, I never wanted to return. Even so, in my absence, I wanted Isabelle to have a better image of me than when I'd arrived.

I looked through my extensive wardrobe, built in my short time at the estate, unsure what would fit the occasion. My eyes fell to the black dress that Edmund handpicked for me what felt like years prior. I only wore it only once and it had found its way to the ground before dinner ended. Of all the dresses I owned, it was by far my favorite. After changing out of my daily attire and into the silken gown, I found Victoria's butterfly necklace and a pair of earrings Sam's wife gave to me when we first met. I never cared for makeup but, in an effort to impress, I dotted my lips with a tinted balm and brushed my cheeks with rouge. It was more work than I ever put into spending an evening with Adrien.

A knock came at my door soon after I finished brushing my hair. My heart pounded against my chest—I was constantly aware of Isabelle's judgment of me. I worried that I went too far.

When I opened the door, my breath caught. Isabelle wore a stunning green gown that matched the color of her emerald eyes. Pale white flowers accented her perfect curves and spilled around her feet. Her hair was down, red curls falling around her shoulders. I wanted so desperately to feel them between my fingers but suppressed my urges. The slight blush of her cheeks and color around her eyes said she'd also taken measures to look her best.

"Well, it seems between us both we'll be attracting a lot of unneeded attention." Isabelle studied me from head to foot. Her stare was absent of its usual chill.

"Isabelle, you look incredible," I exclaimed. "Besides, yours is the only attention I want."

"Josselyn, if you try anything—"

I shook my head and held up a hand. "You're safe with me, my lady. I swear it."

"—Alright." Her lips set into a hard line. "I can't believe I'm doing this."

"If at any point you want to come back, just say the word," I assured her. I turned to take the small leather pouch containing the money Adrien had allotted me.

"That's quite the show back there," Isabelle said. Her tone was somewhere between jesting and curious. I could feel her gaze fixed on my naked back.

"I hoped you could keep an eye on it for me." I paused. "That way you may save me the trouble of such unneeded attention."

When I turned, her face was exactly how I imagined it would look. Torn, confused, embarrassed, unamused. I laughed and walked past her through the door.

"Shall we?" I looked over my shoulder. Isabelle nodded and followed.

There was a chill in the evening air, but it didn't bother me in the slightest. Nothing could with the company of the woman I'd tried to win over for months. Valford wasn't as lively in the evening as Anastas, but plenty of shops were open for us to enjoy. Isabelle never did insist that I buy her new earrings. However, she pointed out to me the expensive perfume that she always wore and I couldn't resist purchasing her a bottle. The shopkeeper assured me that the scent was created using fresh lily-of-the-valley and vanilla. It was sweet, tempting, and an aroma I'd come to associate with Isabelle.

"You didn't have to do that," Isabelle commented for the tenth time, glancing at the small velvet bag she carried.

"I told you, the night is ours. Whatever you want, my lady. Even if it's only a bottle of perfume."

She smiled. It was the first time she'd ever smiled at me. It was perfect, brilliant, lovely. I committed it to memory.

"It's been a long time since I've enjoyed good wine," she remarked. "Would you know where we could buy a bottle or two?"

I returned her smile. "I'm sure we can find something."

We wandered the streets beneath the lights of the shops, keeping a companionable silence that was unfamiliar between us. At last, we came to a shop that specialized in the import of wine and distilled beverages. I led her inside. Every wall was filled to the brim with different vintages and varietals. I perused them in awe. Jeremi and Victoria prized their own specialized cellar where they kept hundreds of bottles for special occasions. They would have adored the convenience of purchasing them so close to home. I wondered briefly what became of their collection.

"What can I help you ladies with?" The shopkeeper eyed us carefully. He was a man who clearly wanted for nothing; plump, rosy-cheeked, and well-dressed.

"We'd like three bottles of your finest red," I replied easily.

"Sweetheart, I don't think you could afford one bottle of my house wine," he blustered.

"And why is that?" I approached the counter leveled my gaze on him.

"Last I knew, a whore's pay wasn't so good," he replied, never flinching.

I took three gold coins from my pouch and placed them on the shop counter.

"And whose pocket did you pick for these?" he asked.

"Will you sell them to me, or not?" I sighed, exasperated.

"From the looks of it, you've already enjoyed all the best bottles yourself." Isabelle's words were cool and even as she picked the gold up from the counter.

"You're a fiery one, aren't you? You must've paid big money for a wisp."

Isabelle's eyes narrowed.

He spared her a dark glare before turning his attentions back to me. "I don't appreciate your kind in my establishment. Anyone who goes against the gods goes against me."

"Let's go, Isabelle. We'll find wine somewhere else," I consented, motioning her toward the door. Like Martin had done on my first visit to Valford, this man assumed my position and was intent on not helping me.

"If you want Lord Markov as your enemy, then so be it." Satisfied with her final retort, we made our way for the exit.

"Wait!" he called after us. "I...I didn't know the two of you...three bottles you said?"

"Three of your *finest* bottles," Isabelle snapped. "On the house."

"Of course, m'lady." Without another question, he disappeared to the back of his shop.

"What a bastard." She sighed.

"This isn't new behavior." I shook my head.

She studied me carefully. I realized she may have taken my comment personally.

The shopkeeper reappeared with three bottles of wine. Two were indeed fine vintages and one was known for its low quality. I couldn't fault him. It was a lot to give away for nothing.

I didn't say anything as Isabelle scooped all three bottles into her arms.

"Thank you for your...understanding." Sarcasm coated her words.

"The pleasure's mine, miss..." He extended his hand in a gesture of companionship.

"Rhodes. Isabelle Rhodes." She glanced at his hand and ignored it, locking her gaze with his until he lowered his arm.

"Lady Rhodes...I had no idea," he stammered.

"Clearly. Come on Josselyn, let's go." Isabelle handed me one of the bottles and we left the building, three bottles richer and not a coin poorer.

"Where should we enjoy these?" I asked. I took a closer look at the bottle in my hands.

"I have an idea. Follow me."

We made our way through the city, only stopping for a moment for Isabelle to buy meats and cheeses from an open stall. She handed the small parcel to me and we proceeded onward, past all of the buildings and storefronts, and up one of the nearby grassy hills. We didn't talk until she finally stopped her deliberate march at the top.

"How do you handle it?" Isabelle broke the silence. She set the bottles down and took a seat in the cool grass.

"Handle what?" I joined her.

"The harassment? The abuse? Not just from that man. I know what I've said to you. I know what the servants say about you. How do you stay sane?"

"I…I don't know." It was the truth.

For harboring such a foul mood, Isabelle had chosen a prime location in Valford. The lights from the town below twinkled, matching the stars above us. A few citizens still wandered the streets, making their way to the tavern. Isabelle opened the first bottle of wine and took a swig before passing it to me.

"The only way to drink good wine, really." I laughed and drank from the bottle as she had. This was one of the better vintages—the shopkeeper did well. It wasn't nearly as good as the red I shared with Cyprus, but Isabelle's company made it all the better.

"He shouldn't have treated you like that," Isabelle concluded, opening the small package of food that she purchased.

"Tell that to all of Rhoryn." I sighed and picked a piece of cheese from the cloth. I handed Isabelle the bottle and she took another few swallows before setting it in between us.

We looked out toward the gleaming lights, passing the bottle back and forth until it was spent. She opened the second bottle and placed it near the food.

"So tell me, Lady Rhodes, about the weight your name carries in Valford." The wine seller's immediate change in tone at the mention of her name did not go unnoticed.

"It's the weight my father carries." She sighed. "He's a prominent bailiff in Rhoryn. He isn't known for his kind sentencing. Everyone has something to hide but, not everyone is willing to die for it."

"That must have been difficult to grow up with," I replied, taking a sip of the newly opened bottle.

"When the man you look up to always has blood on his hands...you don't make a lot of friends."

We shared another silence alongside the wine.

"Josselyn, I...I'm sorry," she said finally.

"Why?" I was stunned at her apology. Never did I imagine Isabelle caring even an ounce for my feelings.

"I've seen you as nothing but a threat ever since you came here. I never gave you a chance."

"What is it you have against Whispers, exactly?"

Isabelle took a long drink from the bottle and refused to meet my gaze. "Many years ago I...I was raped by one."

"Isabelle, I'm so sorry." A piercing cold stabbed my heart. For the second time that week, I contemplated how others viewed our creed. *Love Freely.* I reached for Isabelle's hand and she entwined her fingers with mine.

"It's in the past." She shook her head and looked toward the stars. "My father, he...he had him killed."

"Gods..."

"I've never met one since. I just...I wasn't ready when Adrien brought you to the estate. I was afraid."

"No, Isabelle, I...I didn't even think—" I trailed off. The wine made it difficult to convey my thoughts. "I never imagined..."

"Josselyn, it's okay." Isabelle took another hearty swig of the wine and repositioned herself closer to me. "If it weren't for you, I'd still believe that all Whispers are unfeeling, sex-hungry—"

"I get it." I laughed. With courage that wasn't entirely mine, I laid a hand against her cheek. "I would never do that to you."

"I know," she replied, leaning into my touch. Our eyes locked and an undeniable heat ignited her

When her lips met mine, the world froze. Her kiss was ravenous and sensual, inviting and desperate. Her hands explored my back while I begged for more. The tip of my tongue traced her lips. Before I knew it, my hands were entangled in thick locks of her luscious hair. It was just as sleek and voluminous as I imagined. Isabelle pressed her body against mine and I leaned back onto the grass. Her fingers moved to my hips as she eagerly worked her way deeper into my throat with her tongue. I moaned, her touch sating a desire I'd harbored for months.

Isabelle shifted her mouth to my throat, trailing kisses to my collarbone. I slid my hands from her hair to the small of her back, pulling her nearer to me. Her dress pooled around us both. My heart raced as I kissed her forehead. I couldn't bear to leave her behind...

"Isabelle, come with me," I whispered.

"...What?" She pulled away, breathless.

"I'm...I'm leaving for Anastas. I can't stay here any longer."

"What are you saying?" She distanced herself from me.

I remained lying in the grass, still feeling the heat of her body on mine. I regretted uttering a word. "We can leave Valford. Get away from Adrien. We can start anew." I sat up and took her hand. "I don't want to leave you here with him."

"I can't." Her reply was firm. She removed her hand from mine. "What use do I have in Anastas? This is my home. If Adrien sends my father after me…"

"Then we'll find somewhere else to go. You're knowledgeable in reading, writing, and accounting. We can take enough gold with us that work would be our furthest priority." I thought about my evening in the Cursed Elixir and knew I had at least one contact that could help us. "If I can get in touch with Cyprus—"

"Who's Cyprus?" Isabelle interjected.

I didn't know how to even begin to explain Cyprus. Isabelle saw right through me and said as much. "You met someone when you returned to Anastas, didn't you?"

"Isabelle—"

"Did you let him into your bed, too?" She shook her head. "Is there anyone you *won't* sleep with?"

Her cheeks were flush from wine and her disbelieving stare hurt me to the core. There wasn't anything I could say that would excuse my behavior in her eyes.

"And you speak of Adrien like *he's* a monster." Her disdain for me returned.

I couldn't let her see every Whisper in such a way. What happened to her didn't speak for all Whispers.

"Think of me what you will, but I would never use someone's body for my own gain. I have never tried to twist your perceptions of me, Isabelle, and I never will." I stood up and brushed the grass from my dress. "I…thought you realized my heart could break, just the same as yours…" I felt my shoulders slump. I truly believed she finally saw me in a different light. "As I said before we left, you don't have to stay here with me. We can go back to the estate."

"Wait." She grabbed my hand and held tight to my fingers. "You're right. You haven't forced me to do anything." She pulled me back, glancing at the ground. I seated myself next to her again and she passed me the bottle of wine. "I'm not ready to go back."

"Nor am I, my lady." I laid my head on her shoulder. We spent the remainder of the evening watching the lamps in the city flicker out one by one.

XIV

ver the next two days, Isabelle avoided speaking with me. Occasionally, when she passed me in the hallways, I caught her eye. Color would rise to her cheeks and she looked away immediately. I worried that my attempt to repair her final memories of me were in vain.

At sunset on the eve of my departure, I laid my pack out on the floor of my room and took inventory. It was my first time traveling alone and there was no guarantee I would find Cyprus right away. I needed enough to sustain myself as long as possible. I feared more that when I did find him, he would disappear again.

"You're serious about this."

I looked over my shoulder, meeting Isabelle's steady gaze. She closed my door behind her and joined me on the floor, looking over my travel pack. The soft aroma of her perfume drifted to me and I couldn't help but take a deep breath.

"I can't stay here, Isabelle."

She picked up the sheathed dagger that lay amongst my things.

"Adrien told me you were attacked by bandits on your return from Anastas."

"Yes. I was."

"I'm sure me tearing at your hair afterward did you no favors."

I smirked. "It didn't."

"Aren't you afraid of it happening again?"

"I'm terrified. But, I'm even more afraid of being a hostage to my own desires. I'm afraid of never finding out what happened to my family."

"How will you defend yourself with just a dagger?"

"The dagger isn't for them."

"Josselyn—"

"I will never go back to the City of Ends again." My voice wavered.

Isabelle placed her hand on my shoulder and set the dagger back on the floor. "I've been thinking. About a lot of things. Especially about the other night."

"Did you hate it?"

"No. No, I didn't hate it." She took my hand in hers. I was very aware of her touch. "I wanted to apologize. About something I said. I don't wish you were dead and I'm sorry for your loss."

"Thank you, Isabelle. Truly." I studied her porcelain skin against mine.

"I want nothing but the best for you. I hope you find what you seek."

She kissed my cheek and left as suddenly as she arrived. I stared at my things, wishing I knew the words to say that would convince her to come with me.

Sleep evaded me that evening. Too many worries and thoughts ran circles in my head—never finding conclusions, only more situations to consider. I finally gave up just as the sun peaked over the horizon. I dressed for travel and shouldered the bag I worked so hard preparing for the occasion. Clothes, a blanket, bandages, my book of fairy tales, an extra pair of shoes, and Jeremi's letter would accompany me on my journey. Even though Adrien left me a generous sum of money to do as I pleased, I also stowed away jewelry I could sell if necessary in a small pack hidden beneath my shirt. I took the hooded cloak I wore on my first trip to Anastas and fastened it around my shoulders. I slipped the dagger into my boot, pushing the thoughts of using it away. With a final sweep of the room, I took a deep breath and made my way to the stables.

Besides acting as Adrien's carriage driver, Sam also tended the horses with the care of a mother tending her children. I spent many hours with him learning about each of the inhabitants of the stables and on more than one occasion he gave me riding lessons. I could only hope they would serve me well in my travels.

There was one horse, in particular, I took a shining to and Sam insisted she favored me. A sleek, white, powerful mare that Sam liked to call Princess. In secret, I called her *Elsine,* which was the word for lily in Reln. When Victoria helped me with the gardens, she could never remember the common name for the flower and referred to it in her native tongue.

"Good morning, Elsine," I purred, stroking her strong neck. "Ready for a long day?"

As if she knew my intentions, the mare nuzzled me with her nose.

I found the saddle equipment and readied her as Sam taught me. I contemplated not stealing a saddle, but stealing the horse would be enough to set Adrien fuming—I may as well be comfortable riding. After triple checking the belts around Elsine's stomach, I secured my bag at her neck near the reins. I wanted to be able to keep my eyes on it at all times.

"Josselyn, wait!" My heart stopped at the call of my name. Someone caught me. "You…you were right."

Isabelle. I turned toward her and sighed in relief. She wore the traveling leathers I witnessed her don in my second day at the estate. Her hair was tied back; long, red ringlets flowing over her shoulder. A small pack was bound at her side.

"You startled me." I smiled and helped her pull another saddle from the wall. "Are you sure about this?"

"I'm done acting as a toy...aren't you?" She asked.

"Yes, I am," I replied as Isabelle placed the saddle on a brown and white stallion Sam referred to as King. I hadn't bothered giving the horse a nickname like Elsine—he never took to me as she did. But Isabelle—King caressed Isabelle as if he were her house pet.

"I've never known a horse to be so affectionate." She laughed.

"Seems like you've made a fast friend." I helped Isabelle into her saddle and then moved back to Elsine. "You're positive you want to leave here?"

"Josselyn...I...Let's go." She kicked at King's sides, leading him out of the stables. I encouraged my mare to follow. Isabelle didn't need any more reassurance of her decision; she needed to be free of Adrien's grasp.

"What of the rest of the servants?" I called.

"Don't worry, I took care of it."

We quietly made our way outside of Adrien's estate, down the hills, through the sleeping city of Valford, and onto the open roads that led to Anastas.

I led our journey at a decent speed, having made the trip twice. Isabelle followed alongside me, keeping pace without issue.

"Have you ever been to Anastas, my lady?" I asked once the buildings were far behind us.

"No. My family hails east of Veritas in Maura. I've never traveled this far west."

"You're in for a treat, then." I laughed.

The weather was blessedly cool. A steady breeze kissed our faces as we continued through the forests that led us both to a life unknown.

"Tell me about Cyprus." Isabelle broke the silence previously filled by the morning songs of birds.

"Cyprus…well…he's a Whisper…"

I didn't have to look at Isabelle to know she was rolling her eyes. "Of course he is."

"He's handsome, kind, witty, clever…Actually, I think you two will get along quite well." I laughed. When I thought about it, they had a similar sense of humor that I believed would work as an area of common ground for them both.

She nodded, lips pulled into a tight line. I knew her trust would diminish as soon as I spoke of his race.

"Isabelle, he's passionate about what he loves. In a way I've never seen before," I said.

"That remains to be seen," she replied, her tone flat.

We traveled for a time without speaking, the forest awakening at every turn we made. I kept the knots in my stomach at bay, pushing away thoughts of what Adrien would do to us when he found us gone. Every sound from the woods raised the hackles on my neck. The bandit's cruel smile was still engraved in my mind.

"How did you come to know Adrien?" I asked, attempting to drive away my fears.

She was quiet for a span of heartbeats. "It's a long story."

"We have plenty of time."

"He and my father have known each other for years. I studied astronomy in Myrin for three years before…before I was attacked."

"Is that when you left?"

"Yes. My father and I…have never seen eye-to-eye. I couldn't go back home. Adrien took me in and I've been there ever since."

"Quite the savior, isn't he?"

"So long as it's convenient for him, I suppose." She sighed. "What will we do, once we reach Anastas?"

"There's a tavern there called the Cursed Elixir. We'll start there in hopes of finding Cyprus."

"And if we don't find him?"

"Then we choose a city and get as far away from this place as we can."

"Lucky you have me to guard you, then."

"I asked you no such thing!"

"If I don't, who will?" She caught my eye and kept it. "You, my lady, deserve a better life as much as I."

I felt color rise to my cheeks, dodging the ferocity of her gaze by studying Elsine's mane. "I…I don't think I do—"

"Your heart can heal just the same as mine, can it not?" I chanced a look at her. A wry smile played on her lips and my heart fluttered.

"Yes, my lady, it can." I returned her smile.

Casual conversation filled our journey with ease. The sun shifted from the horizon to midway across the sky. The adrenaline from our escape fueled me without issue until we reached our halfway point. Exhaustion took over me without warning, begging me to sleep if not just for a little while.

"Isabelle…I need to stop." I panted, feeling as though I'd fall off my horse.

"It's alright." Worry tinted her words. "Is there an inn near here?"

I thought of my journeys to Anastas. As far as I recalled, there was no building that could shelter us, even for a few hours.

"Not until we reach the city," I admitted. "Let's pull off the main road and rest."

I led her into the trees and prayed we stay safe while I recuperated.

All that mattered was to find safety for us both in Anastas.

Away from Adrien.

XV

The journey to Anastas from Valford was typically a simple one despite its length. The hills of Valford tapered off into the Verdant Thicket about an hour away from the city. The trees were so old and packed together, that cutting them down to build shops or taverns would cost more than what little foot traffic the path saw. Unfortunately, when attempted on no sleep, not having the option of a place to stay made the trip far more difficult.

"I'm sorry, Isabelle," I muttered for the fifth time as we led our horses through the thick underbrush and trees. My foot slid on a stone that escaped my vision and I nearly lost my balance.

"Josselyn, be careful!" she called from behind me, more concern than I deserved in her tone. I felt like such a fool. "It's alright. I could use a rest, too. As you said, we're halfway there. A little sleep would do us both some good."

I stopped in a small, grassy clearing when I could no longer see the main road. So far, only a handful of merchants passed us by in our travels, but the fear of assailants was ever present. Even if one of us stayed awake to keep watch, we would be no match for a group of men with ill intentions. Thankfully, the foliage was so dense that it covered our newly made trail and blocked us completely from the view of other travelers. I helped Isabelle tie Elsine and King to a sturdy tree branch, giving them plenty of room to graze on the thick grass. The trees made a perfect canopy above us, the sun glittering through their leaves. I began to pull the blankets from our packs while Isabelle wandered ahead.

"Josselyn, look," she called.

Without the noise of the horses' hooves and our idle banter, the sound of moving water mingled with the songs of birds. I shaded my eyes to see what Isabelle discovered. She stood next to a cove constantly fed anew by a babbling stream. It was breathtaking—a tiny, untouched sanctuary amidst the trees. Isabelle bent beside the pond, cupping the clear water into her hands and drinking deeply. Once I situated our blankets over soft patches of grass, I joined her. The day had warmed since we left the estate and the cool drink was most welcome. The surface was like pure crystal; despite its depth, you could see all the way to the bottom. An idea struck me suddenly and I chanced the opportunity.

"Isabelle…" My heart pounded against my chest.

"Hmm?" She glanced at me over her hands.

"I think…it's only fair if I bathe you." I smiled. "To, what was it, atone for my misgivings?"

"In the middle of a forest?" Her eyes widened and her face flushed. Even so, I could tell the idea took hold. "What if someone finds us?"

"We pray they think two beautiful women in a pond is a desperate hallucination?" I laughed.

A curious smile played at her lips.

Thoughts of my hands on her skin softened my tone. "What do you say, my lady?"

She sighed and shook her head. "You're impossible. Turn around."

I did my best to hide my delight and turned toward our blankets. I seated myself on the grass and began to unlace my boots and top. The sun felt wonderful on my bare skin as my clothing slipped away. I folded it and set it beside our packs.

"Alright. I'm ready," she said.

Looking at Isabelle, I had to wonder if I myself was having the desperate hallucination. She stood with one arm across her ample chest, focusing on anything but my face. Her porcelain skin was smooth and perfect. Her red hair fell in stark contrast against her shoulders. The curves that shaped her body were soft and supple and flawless. Standing at the forefront of the pond, she was an absolute vision.

"You look hungry again," she murmured. A blend of unease and longing played at her features.

"And you look heavenly." I took a few cautious steps toward her, doing my best to pace myself. I didn't want to overwhelm her. In spite of my worries, she closed the gap between us. My heart fluttered when her naked skin brushed mine.

"Why so careful, Lady Thorn?" Her fingertips brushed my hair back from my shoulders and crept to my throat. "Lost your nerve?"

I kissed her with a desire I'd withheld for what seemed like ages. She returned it with the same level of ferocity, forcing her tongue into my throat without hesitation. When my hands found her breasts she gasped and tangled her fingers in my hair. Fire danced through my blood and ignited my lust. I guided her toward the cove and I stepped into the water. I gasped from the sudden chill against my heated skin. When my feet hit the smooth bottom of the pool, the water stopped just below my chest.

"Sit," I instructed.

She complied, seating herself on the edge. I pulled her closer so that her calves dangled in the pond. "What about my bath?"

"I haven't forgotten." I laughed and kissed her inner thigh, teasing her skin with my tongue. She was soft and sweet—and I *was* hungry.

"Not just with your mouth, I—" Her comment was cut short when my tongue found its destination between her legs. "Oh, gods…" she breathed, her hands clenching tighter in my hair.

She was already slick with pleasure and I drank her in fervently, grasping at her thighs and drawing her as close to me as I could. She shuddered with every pass of my tongue, her sighs sending shivers down my spine. The taste of her was exhilarating, her body hot and yielding. I moved my hand from her leg and slipped my fingers inside of her, meeting no resistance.

"Josselyn…" My name whispered on her lips was like a song.

I longed for the harmony of her moans.

I synchronized the rhythm of my fingers with the movement of my tongue. Her legs shook, fighting the urge to close around my back. The throbbing against my hand grew more intense as her cries turned desperate. She rocked her hips against me, her hands searching for further purchase in my hair. When the climax took her, the throbs became sharp convulsions and I pushed my fingers as far into her as possible. The erotic sounds that escaped her throat brought my blood to boiling.

I needed her like air.

I pulled away and her gaze met mine—ecstasy painting her features. But her eyes were starving for more. I licked each finger that had been inside her, relishing every drop.

"Get up here." She grasped my shoulders and guided me out of the water, maneuvering herself on top of me. The heat from her body instantly warmed me. Her tongue warred against mine and her fingers found their way inside me. My breath caught and I pushed my hips against her.

"How can you be so…vulgar?" she muttered against my lips.

"It's in my nature." I sighed. "I think you like it."

She smirked and thrust her hand deeper, her kisses mingled with nibbles on my lips. I grasped at her waist, my nails digging into her skin to draw her nearer.

"Isabelle, wait—" I wanted to hold back, to feel her for as long as I could. But servicing her alone had brought me close to climax, and the rhythm of her fingers promised she would have what she wanted.

"Come, Josselyn," she whispered into my ear. "Show me what you're hungry for."

I couldn't stop myself. Her voice stroked me as fiercely as her fingers. I buried my face into her hair, muffling my screams as I orgasmed. I didn't want the entire forest to hear me.

Isabelle kissed me and drew her fingers away. I couldn't find the words to speak but when I did, I felt it was of the utmost importance.

"I...still owe...you a bath," I managed between breaths.

Isabelle laughed and we pulled each other into the pond. I caressed every inch of her skin with a light touch and the chill water, as she did mine. My lips rarely left the company of hers as we cleansed away the memories we left behind.

Once we were satisfied, we left the water and moved to the blankets, basking in the warmth of the sun. I laid my head on her chest as together we looked up at the forest canopy. Isabelle idly brushed her fingers through my hair. I closed my eyes, savoring her touch.

"Josselyn," she murmured lazily.

"Hmm?"

Her fingers entwined with mine. "Thank you."

I fell asleep wondering what I did to deserve her gratitude.

XVI

hen I awoke, the bright sunlight that covered us before was tinted with oranges and purples. We must have slept for hours. Isabelle lay entangled in my arms, her hair a wash of red behind her. She looked more at peace than I ever remembered in my time at the estate. I didn't want to wake her, but we needed to move. It would already be after dark by the time we made it to Anastas. I didn't want to gamble a night out in the forest.

I leaned over Isabelle's quiet form and gently pressed my lips to hers. As she stirred, her arms wrapped around my neck and she pulled me into a deep kiss. Her fingers danced down my spine and I shivered against her touch.

"You really do react to everything, don't you?" she whispered. Her emerald gaze penetrated my thoughts.

"Yes," I admitted. "I…sometimes I…" I wanted to tell her about Adrien, about how he made me wish I was anything but a Whisper. The thought embarrassed me.

"Sometimes what?" She moved an errant strand of hair from my face.

"Sometimes I wish I didn't…react to everything," I admitted.

"Josselyn—"

"We need to leave. It's going to be dark soon and I didn't think to bring lanterns." I reluctantly stood up and fished my clothes from their tidy pile.

"Well, it's a good thing I joined you then. I brought two." Isabelle smiled and stretched before joining me in dressing.

"Ever resourceful, lady Rhodes." I laughed. "My light in the dark."

"I like the sound of that." She kissed my cheek and I felt the blush that hued my face.

We packed the blankets and untied our rested horses. My mind felt clearer and my body rejuvenated. Isabelle seemed more relaxed than when we left and I felt better for it. She took the lanterns from an extra pack tied to King and handed one to me. She tied the other around King's neck.

"Looks like we're ready," she proclaimed. "Let's get out of here."

We waded our way back through the trees and toward the road, keeping the remaining sunlight to our left. Once we found our way out of the forest, we mounted our horses and started at a brisk pace. Isabelle was a far better rider than I, so I asked her to lead the charge. The lanterns she brought served to light our path well after the sun disappeared behind the horizon. No merchants or stray wanderers met us on the rest of our journey and we made great time reaching Anastas.

"Gods almighty," Isabelle marveled when we approached the main square. "Look at this place."

"Welcome to Anastas. To my home." I smiled. We dismounted and made our way into the heart of the city.

The buildings and stalls were alive with lights and crowds; people laughed, cheered, shouted, danced. There was music, the aroma of food, vendors hawking their wares—Anastas was a city that rarely slept. I took Isabelle's hand and held it tightly. With horses in tow, we weaved our way through the clusters of shops and customers alike until I spotted the Cursed Elixir.

"That's where we'll be staying tonight," I called to her over the noise. She nodded in reply and followed my lead.

Arriving at the front of the tavern, we hitched our horses to a post that stood beside a water trough and bale of hay. Hilde was always sweet on travelers and made sure to accommodate everyone—no matter their choice of transportation. I helped Isabelle untie her bag from King's neck before I loosened mine from Elsine's. We walked to the door, avoiding a few lingering couples making their final plans for the evening. The cold metal of the handle was so familiar in my hand—it truly felt like I was where I belonged again.

A warm hand covered mine, causing me to pause.

"I have a better idea of where you could stay," a silken voice murmured into my ear. My breath caught and my hand tightened around Isabelle's.

"Cyprus." I turned toward him. He wore a smile that begged so many questions and his blue eyes were aflame. I didn't care that he left me with nothing but a note. It didn't matter that I thought about him every moment since we'd met.

I missed him dearly.

"Josselyn, love, I'm sorry—"

I cut his words short, letting go of Isabelle's hand to wrap my arms around his waist. I buried my face into his chest and closed my eyes, remembering and memorizing every detail about him I forgot. The scent of his skin, the curve of his back, the sound of his breathing.

He ran his hand through my hair and pulled me closer. "I should be the one groveling at your feet."

"It's...been a long ride." Isabelle's voice broke through my trance.

I pulled away from Cyprus, embarrassed for having not introduced them already. Isabelle's tone was flat. Her gaze settled on mine; knowing and slighted.

"Cyprus Reyner, this is Isabelle Rhodes." I took Isabelle's hand. Her reluctance was obvious, but despite her fears, she shook his hand.

"A pleasure," she said curtly.

"Ah, daughter of Bailiff Garrett Rhodes?" Cyprus eyed her curiously.

"One and the same," she sighed. It seemed to be something she'd heard many times in the past. "Though, don't ask him about me. He'll waste your day telling you how upset he that I'm not a man."

"Well then, my lady," he bent to kiss the top of her hand with a flourish, "let me be the first to tell you that I'm glad you're not."

To my surprise, Isabelle laughed. She took her hand away and glanced at me before looking back to Cyprus.

"You two are so very alike," she said, stifling her laughter. "I understand why Josselyn is so taken with you."

Cyprus replied with a confused smile, shifting his gaze between Isabelle and me.

"We have horses tied up," I spoke up in an attempt to break the tension. Isabelle remained by my side, her hand on my arm. "We need them for wherever we're going."

"Of course." He smiled easily and followed us to the troughs where our horses drank heavily from the water.

"I guess we're not the only ones famished," I commented, feeling my stomach growl in a reluctant reply.

"There's food where we're going, you needn't worry," Cyprus said, helping Isabelle untie King.

I noted her wary glances toward him as he loosed her horse with practiced dexterity. I remembered the kiss of leather knots against my wrists and suppressed the heat that rose to my skin. I undid the coils on Elsine's lines and affixed my bag around her neck once more.

As soon as we were situated, Cyprus led us behind the tavern and stalls, away from the clusters of people. Isabelle followed at a measured pace after him while I trailed behind her. We weaved in and out of alleys and behind stores. Something about our path felt familiar.

"Only a little further," Cyprus called.

It was a beautiful evening. The air was crisp and the stars twinkled their greetings.

"Alright, we're here," he said as our line drew to a halt.

I brought Elsine to the front and fell numb in confusion. I looked between Cyprus, to the estate that stood before us, and then back to Cyprus.

"Welcome home, Lady Thorn," he murmured.

The Terryn estate. My home. I was home.

XVII

nce Isabelle and I bathed and changed from the long journey, we sat in the dining room with Cyprus in silence. My dining room. The space where I once shared countless meals with Jeremi and Victoria. The experience was surreal.

"Josselyn." Isabelle touched my arm. "Are you alright?"

I wasn't alright. None of it made sense. There were too many questions to choose from, all of equal importance—and I couldn't decide what to ask first. I picked at the food that I'd so desperately needed only an hour before. My stomach felt like it was turned in on itself. I didn't know where to begin.

"I…I just…" I started. I didn't want to cry. I wanted to stay numb to the knowledge that, less than four months prior, Jeremi poured me a glass of wine at this table. That Victoria moved her chair inches closer to me so our skin touched while we enjoyed our meal. "I…"

"Let me start, if that's alright." Cyprus' voice interrupted the strings of my memories.

I nodded for him to continue, unsure of what else I could say.

"Victoria and I were…very close. I grew up with her in Lorelyn and we were inseparable. That was, until Jeremi Terryn visited on a business endeavor. They fell in love and left for Anastas within the week. However, she and I kept in touch throughout the years."

"You didn't come back here for work, did you?" I asked, reminded of our first conversation in the Cursed Elixir.

"I came back when Victoria's family notified me of her death. I had to be present for when they read her and Jeremi's last will."

"They…left the house to *you*?" I intended to hide the stab of envy, but my words were sharp. To his credit, Cyprus remained nonplussed.

"Actually, love, they left the house to you." He set his silverware beside his equally untouched plate. "When you were accused of their murder, however, your share went to the next beneficiary listed. Which…was me."

The words weighed heavier on my heart than I expected. Victoria and Jeremi willed their belongings to me. The place I called home for over a decade…it was all supposed to be mine. Additionally, there was one person in all of it that wasn't accounted for.

"Why wasn't Adrien in the will?" I asked.

"Adrien and Jeremi…had a falling out a few years ago." It was Isabelle who answered. "Adrien told me that Jeremi no longer wanted to speak with him. That his own brother betrayed their family. It really upset him."

"Jeremi never said anything about Adrien to me."

"He was probably trying to protect you," Cyprus offered. "Whispers were disappearing and the Temple of Elwyn weren't subtle about their opinions of us."

"How would that protect me? Adrien's his brother."

"Blood relative or not, the less people that knew you're a Whisper, the better," he explained.

"There were many rumors surrounding the Temple a few years ago," Isabelle added. "A lot of the girls in the estate talked about them. Apparently, the clerics were paying good coin for information on the whereabouts of Whispers."

Forever hunted and sold like animals. I shuddered. "Taking all of this into consideration, I still just…Well, they left this all to me and Adrien didn't say a thing." I bowed my head, staring at my hands and giving up my last thoughts of food.

"Josselyn, I intend to change the state of things," Cyprus said. "This is your home and if you don't want me here, I understand."

"That's not it," I replied, agitated that he even asked. Agitated that he could look at me like he was wounded. Agitated that I still had more questions than answers. I found myself toying with Victoria's ring. The ring that Adrien…that Adrien?

"If he wasn't in the will, how did Adrien take *anything* from this estate?" I asked.

"I was informed that three days after the Terryn's murder, Bailiff Garrett Rhodes came to the door with a warrant of execution. It allowed him to collect anything he deemed suspicious." Cyprus sighed. "He couldn't rightfully take the estate or their remaining investments as those were mine in writing—but anything the good bailiff thought pertinent to condemning you as their murderer, he took with him."

"Like I said before, my father and Adrien are very close," Isabelle explained. "Anything in Adrien's possession most likely came from him."

Garrett Rhodes, Adrien, Cyprus…everything was inexplicably connected and I was blind to the path. I shook my head in frustration. Cyprus reached across the table and took my hand.

"May I show you something?" Cyprus asked, standing from the table.

What else was there for me to do? I stood and followed him down the familiar hallways, Isabelle close behind. I touched every portrait, every tapestry, every decoration my fingers could find. I could hear Jeremi and Victoria laughing, talking quietly, calling my name. Their voices echoed against the empty walls, ringing in my ears.

"Josselyn," Isabelle whispered, clasping onto my hand. "Josselyn, don't cry, please."

I didn't register the tears on my cheeks until Isabelle called attention to them. I couldn't stop—it felt like centuries since I'd wandered the hallways I spent more than half my life in. I kept hoping I would find them behind a corner, in one of their favorite alcoves of the house. But only the echoes of memories remained within my heart.

"Here we are."

With both their hands in mine, together they guided me through an open door. It was a room I knew better than any—my chambers. Cyprus hadn't touched a thing. I disentangled my grasp from theirs and moved to explore the last bastion of my family.

Cyprus left everything the way I remembered it. My wardrobe was bare and my jewelry was gone, but the furniture and items that couldn't possibly be used as additions to the murder remained. I tipped a pawn on the obsidian chess set Jeremi gifted me so that we could play together. I never mastered chess as he did, but I took pleasure in finding new ways to outsmart and surprise him. The bookcase I took such pride in stood stalwart in the back of the room; still filled with every volume purchased. My new book of fairy tales would join them soon. And my bed…my bed still had the royal blue quilt and ensconced pillows I remembered so well.

"This is…" I choked on my words. Incredible? Unbelievable? My fingertips made contact with each material, fabric, and piece of furniture. Still, I couldn't bring myself to believe that I was home. Standing in the room I spent thirteen years taking for granted. "Gods…"

"I didn't want to change anything in case you came back," Cyprus said from the doorway.

"Thank you," I whispered. I made my way back to them and collapsed in his arms. Bittersweet sorrow washed over me and I couldn't hold back my cries. "I miss them so much."

"I know, Josselyn." He held me close and I felt Isabelle's reassuring touch on my back. "I do, too."

XVIII

yprus, Isabelle and I lay across my bed side-by-side on our backs. I was positioned between them and took comfort in their warmth. I had finally managed to reign in my emotions and steady my breathing. While I traced the designs of the ceiling with my eyes, a fond memory returned to me.

"I remember…one day Jeremi came home from work with six bottles of wine and a deck of playing cards. He set up a table with a huge plate of food and the drinks in this room, made sure Victoria and I were comfortable, and then ordered the servants to leave us for the night." I smiled, recalling how excited he was.

"What did you do?" Isabelle asked.

"I'm guessing Victoria taught him how to play *Finan,*" Cyprus replied.

"You're right, she did." I nodded. "Jeremi wanted to bring me in on the game—with two new rules."

"How do you play normally?" Isabelle asked, absentmindedly braiding a long section of my hair.

"Each card is assigned a value, and your end goal is to have the lowest score of everyone," Cyprus summarized.

"Seems simple enough. What were the new rules?" She looked at me.

"If you lose, you take a drink of wine." I giggled, ticking the rules off on my fingers. "And if you empty your glass, you lose an article of clothing."

"That's a lot of wine to get through, and not very many pieces of clothing," Isabelle laughed.

"And playing a game that's extremely in Victoria's favor. We played it all the time in Lorelyn." Cyprus said, smiling.

"Learning was easy, mastering it was harder, and I'm certain they let me win more than a few times. We spent the entire night in here, laughing and draining more wine than I think I've ever consumed in my life." I remembered the three of us awoke on the floor the next morning, haphazardly covered in the blankets from my bed. Not one of us remembered how we finished the night. But…that part never mattered. I just wanted to be near them always.

We shared an amicable silence as Isabelle finished the braid and started on another section of hair.

"Cyprus, what happened to your Ring?" I turned my head to look at him. His piercing eyes were concentrated on something above him.

"It's a long story," he replied after a time.

"We all seem to have such long stories," Isabelle quipped.

A smile tugged at his lips, but it was…sad. "Ah, but my lady, it's true." Cyprus touched the tattoo on his finger, still staring upward. "It was a decision I made all too quickly. And for all of the wrong reasons."

"What do you mean?" Isabelle propped herself up on her elbow to see him better.

Cyprus turned on his side so he could see us both. "Becoming a Ring isn't something to be taken lightly. In a failing marriage, there are two people hurt. In a failing Ring, there are three. In the end, a broken Ring holds the same weight as a divorce, if not more." His tone was serious. "Three people must trust each other unconditionally."

"Did her husband not trust you?" I asked.

"That was the curious thing. He trusted me and she didn't." His smile didn't reach his eyes.

"What did you do?" Cyprus had Isabelle's full attention.

"To them? Nothing I wasn't asked. When I discovered that she was convinced he didn't love her anymore? I refused to remain in a place I wasn't wanted. I left."

"Cyprus…" I murmured. I understood the feeling of isolation he carried in his heart. I couldn't imagine the pain of Jeremi or Victoria telling me they no longer trusted me.

"Many Temples of the goddesses will allow you to remarry. None of the Temples who perform Ring ceremonies will allow you to join another couple permanently," Cyprus continued.

"You could just say you're a Ring to another couple, couldn't you?" Isabelle made a valid point.

I opened my mouth to reply, but Cyprus beat me to it.

"You could also 'just say' you're married to someone. Does that hold the same meaning for you?"

She was quiet for a few moments, her eyes searching his face. "No. It doesn't."

There was nothing I could say to ease the heavy feeling in the room. Thankfully, Cyprus changed topics.

"Isabelle, what brought the daughter of a bailiff to the company of two Whispers?"

"Well, you see, it's *such* a *long* story." Her overdramatic tone made me laugh.

"I should have guessed." His smile was easy and disarming.

With very few additional comments from me, Isabelle explained our situation at the Markov estate. How Adrien played us both for fools. That she managed the manor for him in exchange for his help and affections. I was thankful for her omission of the morning I first left for Anastas. I felt guilty remembering my draw to her discomfort with Adrien.

"I'm sorry you've suffered for so long, my lady," Cyprus said once she finished. "You both deserve to be rid of him."

"That's why we're here." I smiled.

Isabelle reached across me and, to my amazement, took Cyprus' hand in hers. She studied the tattoo encircling the base of his finger.

"Your hands are really soft," she commented.

Cyprus laughed. "Why, thank you."

"Josselyn, let me see your tattoo."

I loosed Victoria's ring from my finger and held my hand up to join theirs.

"It's different," she remarked, comparing our hands closely.

"You choose what you want. Usually, all three people help design it," I explained.

"I like them both." She entwined her fingers with our hands. Her skin was cool to the touch.

Cyprus' eyes wandered from our hands to her eyes.

"So, tell me. What is it I'm missing out on?" She asked.

"What do you mean?" I could see what she wanted written all over her face; the fire that glittered in her eyes, the color that hued her cheeks. But, with her wariness of Cyprus, I would not act until she did. Chills raised the hairs on my arms at the thought of enjoying them both.

"What is it like…to have two lovers?" Her eyes avoided ours and she bit her lip as if she wasn't sure where the question came from.

"Well, would you like your description in detail?" Cyprus smirked.

Isabelle shot him an incredulous look. I covered my mouth to keep from laughing.

"Perhaps I could draw you a diagram?" he teased.

"Shut up and show me." She laughed, pulling her hands from ours to grab onto his tunic.

Realizing her intentions, I helped her move him so he lay on her left and she lay between us. It was more of an awkward roll than just moving him and he laughed when he landed next to her.

"You could just ask me to move, you know." His eyes burned, setting my heart alight. "I'm fairly good at following instructions."

"You're incorrigible," Isabelle pulled him to her and sealed his mouth with hers.

I kissed her shoulder, her throat, her cheek, her ear. Ever since our encounter in the forest, I longed for more. She drew away from Cyprus and turned to me, emerald eyes seemingly reading my thoughts. Before I could say anything, her lips claimed mine. Cyprus' arms encircled her waist and his kisses caressed her throat. She eagerly parted my mouth with her tongue and kissed me deeply as he took in the first taste of her skin.

"Is this what you want?" I heard Cyprus mutter into her ear.

"Yes," Isabelle sighed against my lips. "Please."

My fingers delved beneath Isabelle's tunic as Cyprus' arms moved to her hips. I cupped her breasts and teased her hardened nipples with my fingertips. She pressed her chest into my hands and her hips against Cyprus' body. Her moans were intoxicating and only encouraged us both. I slipped her top over her head and Cyprus pulled her skirts to the ground. When her fingers entwined tightly into my hair and her hips rocked backward, I knew Cyprus' fingers had found their target.

"You're soaking wet," he murmured, his voice thick with lust.

I slid my kisses from her mouth, to her ear, to her neck—then Cyprus' lips met mine. Cinnamon and sex; exactly as I remembered.

He pushed his tongue down my throat, his free hand supporting the back of my neck. I gasped when I realized Isabelle had slipped her hands beneath my own tunic to reciprocate my affections. Her dexterous fingers caressed, pinched and coaxed my breasts. Her teeth sunk into my shoulder and I shuddered, my body melting into hers. Moaning against Cyprus' mouth, I tore at his clothes and his hands moved from his attentions to join Isabelle's in removing my own. In a matter of heartbeats, we were all vulnerable to each other. We shifted positions to the floor, Isabelle's ivory skin striking and lovely against our darker tones.

My heart raced as my breathing hastened. The feel of their skin against mine, the suffocating heat that emitted from all of us; I'd desperately missed the feel of two lovers.

"Gorgeous," I marveled, pulling her on top of me.

Cyprus followed us, kneeling closely behind her back.

"I wish I could mark every inch of you," I crooned.

"I'll help you with that," Cyprus growled, kissing and nibbling small sections of the soft flesh trailing her spine.

I mimicked his movements down the front of her body; beginning with her throat, moving to her breasts, then to her stomach, and pausing at her hips.

"Please...." Isabelle begged as I grazed her upper thighs with my tongue.

She pressed her hips against my mouth and I couldn't help but answer her plea. I positioned her above me and slid my tongue between her folds. She cried out and bucked into me. I grabbed her thighs in response and set her grinding to my desired pace. Cyprus' lips had moved to my skin, lingering at my breasts before traveling down my stomach. Then my hips, then the apex of my pleasure. The warmth of his breath and deliberate strokes forced me to moan against Isabelle. Her whole body shuddered in response.

The taste of her, the feel of him, their cries of ecstasy with mine. I wanted to drown in that moment.

I felt myself inch closer to climax and moved my hands from Isabelle's thighs to her hips, encouraging her to turn the other direction. She understood and did as I beckoned, the heat of Cyprus' breath disappearing. I didn't need to utter a word; he understood what I wanted.

When he entered me, my entire body shook with need. I pressed my hips against his while I worked Isabelle incessantly with my tongue. I heard his lips meet hers. Three people—no one lost, no one forgotten. It was a liberating feeling not easily explained, only experienced.

One pair of hands found their way to my chest as another clasped around my hips.

"I'm going…to…" Isabelle panted with an urgency that quickened my tongue.

Cyprus thrust deeper into me. Faster. Pulling my thighs higher. Positioning my calves against his shoulders. When Isabelle orgasmed, her cries were high and desperate. I drank her in while Cyprus continued his intense rhythm. Isabelle bent her mouth to my hips, her tongue gliding over my skin, up to my navel.

"Josselyn, come for me." Cyprus' voice drifted to me from somewhere far away.

My body responded without question, convulsing around him while Isabelle lapped and bit at my flesh. I cried out against her thigh as Cyprus climaxed and the sighs of his apex joined my own.

For a moment, the three of us were still, only the sounds of our heavy breathing filling the room. At last, Isabelle slid to my left side and Cyprus moved to my right. We lay together on the carpet in the moonlight, descending from the high.

I knew Cyprus and I wanted to go further. We were Whispers. This was nothing. But, Isabelle...

"Isabelle?" I turned to her and Cyprus curled his body against mine in response, wrapping his arms around my waist and kissing my shoulder. He was far from sated. "Are you alright?"

She turned to me. A half smile curved her full lips and satisfaction glittered in the green sea of her eyes. "I could get used to this." Her mouth found mine and she pressed her entire body against me. Her fingertips drifted over my skin and behind me to Cyprus.

He moaned and reached one arm across me for her. They had me locked in between their embrace. Isabelle could keep pace with us—she burned for our touch as we did hers and we would savor it.

The three of us spent hours in my room exploring one another until exhaustion took us all. It was something I never fathomed I would experience again after Jeremi and Victoria. A void that I hadn't realized I harnessed was suddenly filled.

I loved them both. And I feared what would come of it.

XIX

While Cyprus and Isabelle dozed soundly in my bed, I found myself sleepless and wandering my room. I dressed in Cyprus' tunic, hugging it close to my body and inhaling his scent. I padded barefoot against the soft carpet, relearning every nook and cranny of my quarters. I finally took a seat at my favorite piece of furniture—an ebony vanity with intricate flowers and vines carved into the mirror and legs. It seemed to survive untouched, and the simple fact that it remained was something I took solace in. On my sixteenth nameday, Victoria convinced Jeremi to help her gift it to me. She claimed that any self-respecting young woman had her own vanity. Once I caught wind of her idea, I supported it wholeheartedly, slipping it into casual conversation whenever I could. Of course, Jeremi couldn't refuse our pleas; he never denied us anything, no matter how trivial.

One of my favorite aspects of the vanity was a set of compartments Jeremi requested be installed on the surface. They were barely visible to the naked eye and could only be opened from a latch beneath the edge of the mirror. My fingers danced beneath the carvings until I felt it and I unhooked the fastening as easily as I'd done just a few months prior. Sliding the square of ebony away revealed what I knew I left beneath it: a leather-bound journal that Jeremi purchased for me when he taught me to read and write. He encouraged me to relive my thoughts and feelings in a place that was mine and mine alone. Unfortunately, I fell out of the habit of writing shortly after my Ring ceremony. I held every memory of the Terryns dear and wondered if I should document them as I once did.

I lifted the book from its home and dusted off the flat, black cover before thumbing through dates and memories beginning from the time I was fourteen. I was able to see the steady progress I made from my first written letters, to my name, to full sentences of thought. I smiled at the obvious places where Jeremi steadied my hand, or Victoria added a note here and there. As I reached the end, a piece of parchment slipped from the back cover and onto the floor. I wondered if the binding had withered over time as I retrieved the paper, but unfolding it revealed a document larger than the pages of my journal.

CITY OF ENDS AUCTION AGREEMENT

On this 24th day of the Sixth Month, I, Jeremi Terryn, agree to pay the total sum of 50,000 gold for one, Josselyn Thorn, Lot 7. Payment signifies the end of the current ownership of this person(s) held by Rochefort and Markov. By signing this document, I retain all rights to my winnings and abdicate the previous owners, auction house employees, and clerics of the faith from any responsibilities of the named person(s).I agree to not disclose the terms and conditions of this contract, as well as the details surrounding the auction. By signing, I understand that any found in breach of this contract may be subject to: forfeiture of purchased property, financial compensation, seizure of all assets and commensurate punishment as set by the auction house.

As I unfolded the last section to reveal Jeremi, Adrien and Bastion's signatures, a carefully pressed lily fell into my lap.

Elsine. Victoria. A numbing cold seeped through my veins as I re-read the contract.

Seizure of all assets…

Jeremi had left the document for me on purpose. In a place where he knew no cleric, bailiff, or even his own brother would look.

Commensurate punishment…

What went so terribly wrong? Whatever it was, he and Victoria underestimated what would happen to me if I survived.

Bastion Rochefort and Adrien Markov had followed through on their contract.

XX

awoke in a room that was painfully familiar. Ivory sheets and pillows covered the bed, decorated with green, patterned embroidery that I traced with my fingertips. I didn't remember moving to Jeremi and Victoria's room—I still clutched the contract of sale and dried lily to my chest like lifelines. Despite the damp trails of skin on my cheeks revealing that I'd cried myself to sleep, I felt more rested than I had in days.

"We were worried about you." Isabelle's voice came from behind me.

I turned to see her and Cyprus sitting on the floor next to the bed.

"I…I didn't want to wake you. I know you needed the sleep." She was holding his hand.

When I attempted a reply, my throat was scratched and hoarse. I swallowed and tried again, my voice still weak. "You don't have…to sit on the floor." I managed a smile, but inside I felt empty.

"Josselyn, what's wrong?" Cyprus stood, helping Isabelle to her feet. They both approached, worried and seemingly afraid to touch me.

"This whole time…it was Adrien this whole time." I offered Cyprus the contract.

He scanned it before handing it to Isabelle, color draining from his face.

"I'm an idiot," I groaned.

"Gods…this is…" Isabelle sat beside me, abashed. "You were auctioned? Sold like livestock? What in the seven hells…"

"Adrien Markov and Bastion Rochefort run the entire operation. I knew Rochefort was purchasing young men and women to sell but this…This is far worse than I imagined." I held the pressed lily between my fingers, studying its delicate petals and leaves.

"Where did you find this?" Cyprus looked over the paperwork again.

"There's a small compartment in my vanity where I kept a journal. Jeremi and Victoria knew about it and left it there," I replied, twirling the flower.

"I'd keep it in that compartment for now. We don't want this falling into anyone else's hands." Cyprus handed the contract back to me and positioned himself beside me. He stroked my hair as Isabelle entwined her fingers with mine.

"There's…one thing I can't make sense of," I admitted.

"Hmm?"

"There were other documents I found in Adrien's study—" I started but Isabelle interrupted me.

"How did you get in there?" Her eyes widened.

"He was…occupied." I couldn't bring myself to say it out loud, but the blush on her cheeks said she knew. "Anyway, one was for the original sale from my parents to Rochefort. The other was for Adrien posting my bail from the Temple of Elwyn, also signed by Rochefort. Why did Adrien need to pay for me twice?"

"Perhaps Rochefort gave that money back? He may have wanted to create a paper trail." Cyprus suggested. "I would imagine if someone like Rhodes showed up at the Temple demanding paperwork on your release, he would want some proof of bail."

"That money never returned to his account," Isabelle pointed out. "I handled all of his finances, including the bail."

"They originally purchased me from my parents for a thousand gold," I explained. "Jeremi paid fifty thousand, and Adrien nearly quadrupled that amount to get me out of prison. Why did Rochefort charge so much? I imagine you wouldn't want to fleece your business partner so terribly?"

"That's a good question," Cyprus agreed.

I didn't know what else I could say. There was nothing that could really be done for it. I felt helpless and hopeless, but their touch was enough to hold me together.

"I gave myself to a murderer," I murmured. "Adrien had a hand in every aspect of my life."

"I know this isn't the most comforting thought, but without him, you never would have met Jeremi and Victoria. Or…Isabelle and I," Cyprus replied.

And without him, they would still be alive. I thought bitterly. *Without me, they might still be alive.*

"I have one more piece of paperwork you should see. I understand how you must be feeling, but I think it's necessary," Cyprus said, standing from the bed. He left the room and Isabelle took his place running her free hand through my hair.

"What…what was the auction house like?" she asked cautiously.

"Do you remember the day I was screaming in my sleep?" I had no desire to retell the tale of that particular hell. Not now.

"Yes…"

"It…was like that." I tried to keep my tone more blunt than angry.

"I-I'm so sorry, I—" she stammered, color rising to her face.

"No, I'm sorry, Isabelle. I just can't." I sighed and moved my head to rest on top of her thigh. "I promise to tell you one day."

"I understand." She squeezed my hand. "I just can't believe a place like that exists…"

"Neither could I," I replied quietly.

Cyprus returned moments later with the aforementioned document. Retaking his place beside us, he handed the parchment to me. It was Jeremi Terryn's will.

"I suggest reading it from the beginning," he said.

I sat up and brushed the hair from my face, heart racing. I read it aloud for Isabelle's benefit.

"'I, Jeremi Terryn, a resident of the city of Anastas in the Kingdom of Rhoryn, being of sound mind and memory, do hereby make, publish, and declare this to be my last will and testament. All references herein to "this Will" refer only to this last will and testament.'" I paused and glanced at Cyprus.

"Keep going."

"'At the time of executing this will, I am married to Victoria Terryn, and bound by sworn oath of communion to our Ring, Josselyn Thorn. All holdings belonging to me registered under the following name shall also be distributed to my inheritors: Jeremi…'" I stopped reading. I couldn't comprehend the words in front of me.

"What does it say?" Isabelle shifted to look over my shoulder.

"…Markov. Jeremi Markov." I shook my head, realization dawning on me. "Adrien didn't change his name. Jeremi did."

"There's…one more part you should read." Cyprus pointed lower on the paper, and I continued.

"'I specifically, intentionally, and with full knowledge, fail to provide for Adrien Markov in this will.'" I handed the document back to Cyprus. "Jeremi didn't just leave Adrien out of the will. He barred him from any of his holdings."

I couldn't take any more new information—it was all too much to bear and I felt near to bursting. I stood up from the bed and took my leave of the room. "I need a moment alone."

"Josselyn, wait!" Isabelle called, but I heard Cyprus convince her to stay.

Isabelle had said Jeremi and Adrien suffered a falling out three years before. From Jeremi's name change and his last will, this wasn't a simple falling out. This was a war.

And at the center of it all was me.

XXI

I went to my room and pulled a book from my shelf. It was the collection of stories Victoria would read to me before I fell asleep. I needed to hold on to a memory that wasn't Adrien's hands against my skin. As I made my way outside, I averted my gaze from the walls with their familiar tapestries and paintings. I slowed when I made it to the gardens, collapsing onto the grass on my back and closing my eyes.

The songs of birds accompanied a gentle breeze. The warm sun felt divine on my face. For a handful of seconds, time stood still, and nothing was amiss. I hugged the book to my chest and clung to that small span of peace.

"May I join you?" I didn't hear Cyprus approach, but his voice never seemed to startle me.

I nodded, not ready to open my eyes. He lay beside me in the soft grass. Tenderly weaving one arm beneath my waist, he encircled the other around me. I lay the book aside and turned into him, burying my hands and face into his tunic. The gentle caress of his lips brushed against my throat.

He held me in silence for a long time, the sun warming my back and his steady heartbeat slowing my breaths.

"Josselyn...I'm sorry," he whispered. "I should have never left you alone in that tavern."

"Why did you?" I was thankful for the change in subject, but this one was nearly as difficult.

"I was a coward." He rested his chin on the top of my head. "Every rumor and shred of news carried around Anastas painted you as Victoria and Jeremi's murderer—"

"That night…you already knew who I was," I realized. Cyprus said it himself; he returned to Anastas for the reading of their will. "You knew who I was and you took me to bed anyway."

He'd lied to me. My stomach turned. He knew my past, inherited my future, and Victoria never so much as uttered his name.

"I should have explained everything to you right away. I was a fool not to trust you." He kissed my forehead and tilted my chin up so we met each other's eyes. "That morning, I was scared I'd made a mistake. That my confidence was ill-placed."

"But you left me Victoria's necklace," I said, unmoved.

"And apparently her ring." Cyprus took my left hand and toyed with the ring Adrien had passed on to me. "This was a wedding gift from me to her. I didn't think she would hold onto it for so long…"

"Cyprus…" The longing that coated his words tore at my heart.

"I wanted to give you something that would make you want to come back. You deserved so much more, but the necklace was all I had." He sighed. "I hope you can forgive me."

I couldn't help but laugh. Understandably, he looked confused. He hadn't the slightest idea of how much I missed him when I returned to Adrien.

"I forgave you the moment I stepped foot back in Valford." I touched his cheek with my fingers, drowning in his gaze. My lips met his in a long, tender kiss. No lust or hidden motives hid beneath it—only pure affection. I wrapped my arms around him and held tight. In his arms, I felt safe. I felt complete. What terrified me was losing that feeling all over again.

"I…I have to go back," I murmured against his mouth.

"What?" Cyprus leaned away, eyebrows knitting together.

"Adrien will come back from Veritas to find Isabelle and I missing. He'll hunt us down. I can't let him hurt either one of you." I bowed my head. "I can't…"

"Then let me come with you," he said. "We'll end this together."

"I don't want to risk that—"

"Josselyn, I let you go once. Please don't make me do it again." His hand drifted to my cheek. "We need to talk to Isabelle about all of this before we make a decision. I believe you would hurt her more by leaving her here without a word."

He was right. I saw it in the way she stood guard of me when we returned to Anastas. At some point in our relationship, Isabelle had become protective of me in ways I never imagined possible. I wanted nothing more than to return the favor.

"Alright," I conceded. "If you don't mind, though…I'd like to stay like this for a little longer."

"Of course, love." He touched his forehead to mine. "As long as you wish."

I leaned into another deep kiss, savoring every moment we shared together.

I wouldn't lose him again.

"Are you insane?" Isabelle gawked at me from across the dining table. "There's nothing there for us, Josselyn. And gods forbid he realizes we left without permission—"

"That's just it. He's going to return to his estate and find us gone. What do you think he'll do then?" I swirled my glass of wine and nibbled on a piece of bread.

She was silent, contemplating my question.

"Do you think he'll allow the Whisper he sold and the servant with extensive knowledge of his trade to simply go free?"

"…No. He'll find us. No matter where we hide," she admitted.

"We have a few documents that already show Adrien's involvement in the auction. There has to be something that condemns him for good," Cyprus offered, pouring more wine into Isabelle's glass.

"I…I think I know where he keeps some of the letters from my father," she said carefully. "If I can get my hands on those, they might have more information about what exactly happens at the auctions."

"Do you think your father knows of these auctions?" I asked.

"To buy and sell so openly, I believe Lord Markov would need the assistance of the guard." Cyprus shrugged. "If they're as close as Isabelle says, all the more reason to believe it."

"I would run missives back and forth between them often. The first time you and I met, it was on my return trip," Isabelle explained. "He saved many of the letters in a separate place from his study."

I nodded. "I saw where he keeps my papers from my original sale, which would seal Rochefort's fate. If we get back before he returns from Veritas, we can search the estate for all the things he's kept from us."

Cyprus took a hearty drink from his glass. "If we find enough damning paperwork against him, we can take it to the barrister in the Capital. It would be going above the bailiff's head, but I think it's a risk we have to take."

A pained look crossed Isabelle's features. "Knowing my father's history with Adrien, I fear he would turn a deaf ear. No matter which one of us presented it to him."

"Then that's what we do." I nodded. "We have at least a few days before Adrien returns. We should depart soon."

"The more servants we can avoid, the better. Every one of them acts like a spy," Isabelle said, rolling her eyes.

"Then we'll go after dark," I said.

Cyprus and Isabelle nodded.

All three of us picked at our food and sipped the wine. The tension in the room was cloying.

"Cyprus, Isabelle," I muttered. "Thank you."

"We'll prove to him we're a force to be reckoned with; that we're far more than just his playthings," Isabelle's reply was quiet. Even so, her entire demeanor changed to one of determination.

"We are. And we will." I took her hand and Cyprus'.

We were prepared to stop Adrien Markov, no matter the cost.

XXII

espite the aching in my thighs from more horseback riding than I ever experienced in my life; Isabelle, Cyprus and I raced to Valford.

We had packed only what we needed to for a brief rest in a nearby town. Then we would make straight for the Capital with whatever paperwork we could find in Adrien's estate.

We ran our horses ragged, pausing a few moments for water and a short rest. The three of us exchanged very few words; all of us mentally readying ourselves for the task at hand. In order to stay ahead of Adrien, we would have to move quickly.

The hour was well past midnight when we reached Valford. Not a soul remained on the road and the estate was deathly quiet. I wasn't sure who took charge of the manor's affairs while Isabelle was gone. I hoped whatever excuses she created held fast.

"It looks like Lily didn't destroy the place," Isabelle murmured as if answering my thoughts. "That girl could burn a pot of water, but she manages everything else pretty well."

Cyprus chuckled underneath his breath.

"We should stop here," I suggested, still far from the estate.

There was a signpost showing passersby the way around town. Isabelle proposed we tie our horses to it so they didn't make any unneeded noise. Cyprus and I agreed. We dismounted and made the rest of the journey to Adrien's estate on foot. Isabelle led us around the back, stopping when we came to a set of wooden doors angled against the ground. She briefly searched her pack before revealing a set of keys.

"This leads into the pantry where we keep preserves and bulk food. There's a door that opens into the kitchen from there," Isabelle explained in hushed tones. "All the girls should be gone by now, but a few like to stay here overnight when Adrien is gone, so keep your voices down."

"What do we do for light?" I asked. The moon was bright, but as soon as we made it in the basement it would be pitch black.

"There should be a spare lantern or two down there. I know every brick in this place, so I'll go first," she replied.

"Isabelle, be careful," Cyprus cautioned.

She blushed and nodded before descending the stairs.

Cyprus and I waited quietly, the seconds stretching on like years. My heart pounded against my chest and I worried the whole world could hear it. When I considered calling out to make sure Isabelle was alright, a circle of light illuminated her upper body.

"There're only two lanterns down here," she announced.

"Then we'll split up," I replied, using the dim light on the stairs to guide me down to where Isabelle stood. Cyprus followed closely behind.

"Where do we start?" Cyprus asked, igniting the other lantern.

"I'm going to give the room I stayed in one more look and then I'll move to the study where I know the paperwork is." I wondered if Adrien would have kept anything in plain sight of me the whole time. Regardless, it was worth checking.

"The letters from my father would be in his chambers, and he may have left a few in mine by accident," Isabelle replied.

"You and Cyprus should stay together. If one of the servants who stayed catches you, you'll be able to explain his presence much better than I can." All of the girls knew that I shared

Adrien's bed. Another man at my side at this hour would raise too many questions.

"Will you be alright on your own?" Cyprus asked, but they both looked worried.

"I'll be fine." I offered a smile, but my racing pulse said otherwise. I kissed both of their cheeks and made my way up to the kitchen. "As soon as you find what you need, meet me back here."

They nodded and watched me go, giving me a head start down the hallway. Two lanterns in the same room or hallway could attract unwanted attention.

I silently made my way to what were my chambers and slipped through the door. I felt like an intruder in what I considered my room just a few days prior. Everything was just as I left it, down to a few stray books that lay open on the bed. I sorted through the drawers of my wardrobe and searched the compartment of my nightstand. Nothing. Every time I thought I heard a noise I started in fear. I had to get a hold of myself.

I moved to the bookcase. I flipped through the pages of each tome and checked in between the bindings for any paperwork or documents pertinent to our cause. Still, I found nothing. I wasn't surprised, though a small part of me hoped there would be just a shred of evidence that he left in that room.

I put everything back in its place and returned to the hall, closing the door so it wouldn't make a sound. Adrien's study was a fair way down from my room. Thankfully, Isabelle was right—no servants patrolled the halls this late. I finally reached the heavy door and entered in silence. Moonlight lit the room as it did for me before. I held my lantern close and moved to the desk that I knew held the final blow to put a stop to Adrien Markov. The lock that was once open to me was fastened tight around the drawer I needed. I should have expected as much. I stood to search for a heavy enough object to break it with.

"Welcome back, Josselyn." His voice startled me to shrieking. He lit the lamp at the door, illuminating the room. Adrien.

"How did you...you weren't supposed—" I stammered, backing up to the window.

"To be here? No, I wasn't. But, one of the ladies thought it wise to notify me immediately when the Whisper and my head servant left without warning." He approached me, glancing at his desk. "And what were you looking for in there?"

I couldn't breathe. Everything we planned...I couldn't let him find Isabelle and Cyprus.

"I just...Adrien I..." I didn't know what to say. I couldn't tell him the truth. I left the remaining paperwork with Elsine and I prayed he hadn't found her, too.

"To think I trusted you enough to leave you alone for a few days. Not only do you leave, but you took Isabelle with you?" He snatched my wrist and squeezed. "What an insufferable little cunt."

His fingers hurt. Anger boiled over my fear. "You won't be able to sell people for gold much longer—"

"My lord, we found these two in your chambers," another voice came from the entrance.

Two large men stood in the doorway, forcefully holding Cyprus and Isabelle captive. When the light hit their faces my heart stopped. Finn and Isaac. Adrien's corruption reached so much further into my life than I imagined.

"No..." I murmured.

Cyprus struggled furiously against Finn while Isabelle seemed to have lost consciousness in Isaac's arms.

"Good to see you again, darling." Finn's lips twisted into a smile. "Don't worry about my sword. I'll be buying a new one after this."

"So, you were saying, sweet?" Adrien tangled his hand in my hair. "We'll talk more when you wake up."

Before I could say another word, he thrust me down until my head smashed into the desk. White pricks of light penetrated my vision.

Cyprus screamed my name and I knew no more of the world.

XXIII

onsciousness returned to me in slow, painful pieces. My head throbbed, pulsing in rhythm to the ringing in my ears. Warm, sticky, liquid anchored my hair to my head, dripping down to stick errant strands to my face—blood. My arms were strained, wrists burned, and whatever surface lay beneath me was ice cold. When the dark spots finally cleared my eyes, the grievous scene illuminated before me had me holding back screams.

I was in a small room I didn't recognize as any part of Adrien's estate. Cyprus was down on his knees, clothes torn, hands bound behind his back, eyes set to the floor. Blood dripped through his hair and down his face. Isabelle lay beside him, dress in tatters, eyes closed, and body unmoving. Her feet were tied in addition to her hands. Her skin looked impossibly pale. I couldn't tell if she was breathing. My heart stopped.

"Isabelle!" Only then did I realize how futile struggling was. My wrists were also bound, but spread diagonally from my body and pulled to opposite ends. I had been stripped to nothing. My entire upper body was stretched across a table, naked skin chaffing against the wood. My feet were square on the freezing ground.

"She's alive, I assure you." Adrien's velvet voice came from beside me. "Once we're done here, though, that may change."

Memories from the City of Ends rushed back to me. Being forced into the same vulnerable position, the people along the walls watching me raped and tortured. I thrashed against the ropes; panic consumed me and desperate cries ripped from my throat.

"I hope you're comfortable," Adrien spoke over my screams. "We have a lot of things to talk about."

"Then let her off the table," Cyprus growled. "Unless you're afraid of what she'll do to you when you let her go."

Tears mixed with blood, streaking my face as they fell. I was hyperventilating. I tried my best to catch my breath, terrified of losing consciousness again. I feared never waking up.

"This isn't about me fearing Josselyn. Quite the opposite actually. It seems she never learned to fear me," Adrien replied easily.

"Adrien, please let me go," I whimpered. It was my worst nightmare. Our plan went completely awry. None of us had accounted for Adrien returning early. Isabelle and I were so sure the servants were unaware of our true intentions.

Cyprus met my gaze—dark bruises and deep cuts penetrated his skin, trails of blood seeped to his throat. Despite the pain he suffered and the situation we found ourselves in, the determined fire he carried was still there in his eyes. I clung to it—my life depended on it.

"Why don't we start with…whatever this is?" Adrien motioned back and forth from Cyprus to me while he leaned against the table. "Who are you, exactly?"

"That doesn't concern you," Cyprus barked.

"I beg to differ." Adrien moved from the table to where Cyprus knelt. "And I have all night to find out."

Cyprus gasped as Adrien's leg connected with his stomach. He groaned and doubled over, sputtering blood onto the floor. It took every ounce of will in my body to not call out to him.

"I've met barmaids more intimidating than that." Cyprus laughed. "You're going to have to try harder."

"We'll see what you say after you're less a finger or two." Adrien moved to the table momentarily to lift a large knife I didn't see before. It shined gruesomely in the dim light.

Cyprus' delicate hands. His life once depended on them and Adrien had no idea.

"Adrien, stop it," Isabelle rasped, looking up at him from the floor.

"Ah, my little rose is awake." Adrien crouched. He caressed Isabelle's enraged face, still clutching the knife. "You'll answer my questions, won't you, sweet? Like you always have?"

"You're a monster." Her voice regained its strength. "You murdered Josselyn's family, didn't you?"

"My own brother? I would never." His offense was clearly feigned. "No, love. Your father took care of that for me."

"My...father?" Isabelle's eyes widened. It seemed as if time paused around us, allowing Isabelle and I both to comprehend his words. "But he...no. You're lying."

Adrien shrugged. "You helped him, pet. All of the missives you delivered to him for me—he never could have done such a flawless job without them."

Isabelle had guessed correctly. There *was* something in those missives to condemn Adrien. Far more than we expected. It made perfect sense—Adrien could pay Garrett to reclaim me due to the ridiculous violation of their contract.

"Lord Rhodes is a perfectionist when following through. But you knew that when he killed Sylus, right Isabelle?" Adrien taunted her. "It takes a lot of power to murder a Whisper in another Kingdom."

"Do you always hide behind the people who do the dirty work? You're a goddamn coward," Cyprus spat.

Adrien struck Cyprus against the ear with the hilt of the blade before moving behind him. Adrien's hands worked where I could not see.

Cyprus' muffled cries were enough to force my words. I couldn't let Adrien hurt him anymore. I wouldn't stand by and watch—not now, not ever.

"Adrien, stop!" I yelled. "His name is Cyprus. Cyprus Reyner."

To what I could only imagine was everyone's shock, Adrien laughed. It chilled me to the bone. He moved away from Cyprus, placing the knife on the table and standing beside me once more.

"What's so damn funny?" Isabelle spat.

"Cyprus. The wisp that chased after my brother's wife without end?" Adrien scoffed. "How did it feel? Losing her to a better man?"

Cyprus had said that he and Victoria were close—never that he harbored feelings for her. Just as I thought I found the answers to my questions, only more were created. Why did Adrien know things about my family that I didn't?

"You're twisting Jeremi's words," Cyprus hissed. "You have no idea what I've suffered—"

"Rhodes told me that killing her was the easiest thing he's ever done. Like she was waiting for it," Adrien reminisced as if recalling a fond memory. "I wonder what she thought about in those last moments. Or who…?"

"Stop it!" I screamed, fighting against my restraints.

Outrage colored Cyprus' cheeks. Immense pain overtook his features.

"Why? Why did you want them dead?" Isabelle demanded.

"Jeremi wanted nothing to do with the family business. I respected him for that and took it over in his stead—"

"You place a price on people!" I shouted. He spoke of it with such nonchalance that I couldn't help myself.

Without missing a beat, he struck me across my unprotected face. Stars glittered in my vision and I struggled to keep focus.

"As I was saying. Jeremi and I were still very close. Even after he changed his name to try to escape his heritage and then married Victoria, we still spoke and met often. But when they decided to make you their Ring—" Adrien looked pointedly at me— "he became a lot more...opinionated."

I wanted to say something, *anything,* to debunk his story, but I wasn't sure if I would be able to sustain another blow.

"Suddenly, the trade that keeps me alive wasn't morally correct—our family was in the wrong all these years. I needed to take the 'high ground' and close it down. All because they purchased a wisp from the City of Ends." He took the blade and twirled it against the wood, dangerously close to my wrist. Cyprus' blood stained the sharp edge of the steel.

I wondered what changed Jeremi's mind. Was it truly me?

"My father wouldn't kill for something so...so trivial!" Isabelle snarled.

"And that's where you're wrong, sweet. Bailiff Rhodes has stakes in those auctions equal to mine and word of them getting to the people above him...well, he couldn't risk that," Adrien retorted.

It fit into the picture. Every piece of the puzzle Adrien supplied worked exactly where I was missing information. My wrists and fingers began to lose feeling. The restraints cut off my circulation.

Adrien laid the knife near my arm and stroked his fingertips across my breast.

I shivered and hated myself for it.

"At first, I instructed Rhodes to kill all of you. I didn't have a use for some tart my brother called a Ring. But then…" He smiled.

My stomach twisted.

His fingers moved to trace my collarbone. "A certain tavern owner told me about the Whisper they loved."

"Hilde," I murmured. She must have been taken with Adrien's charm immediately. Even so, he said it himself. He never wanted Jeremi's Ring…

"You paid the Temple for me because you were *curious*?" I said, not caring if he hit me. At that moment, I would have gratefully taken the pain over the complete awareness of his fingertips tracing my skin.

"Rochefort is a greedy son of a whore." Adrien sighed. "Rhodes was the one who thought to frame you and bring you into Rochefort's hands. That secured you a room in the Temple of Elwyn's dungeons for me to come release you. Rochefort took advantage of the situation. But, there were some things I needed to destroy first."

"Rhodes didn't search the Terryns' manor to condemn Josselyn…he was looking for the contract," Cyprus deduced.

"Perceptive, aren't you? Most customers of the auction house destroy their paperwork. I know my brother better than that. No matter now, the only ones who know will soon be taken care of." His hand slid down the curve of my back and I shuddered.

"That's the last letter you had me bring to my father. You told him not to kill her." Realization dawned on Isabelle's face. "The day I came back…the day Josselyn was here…"

"As I told you, Isabelle. I needed you." Adrien smirked. "But that time is at an end."

"You can't kill me. My father will have your head." Isabelle's voice shook with something beyond anger.

"I don't think so. Here's the way I see it. I came home from Veritas to find you and Josselyn dead. Thankfully, my servants managed to capture your murderer, Cyprus Reyner, and I exacted the vengeance you both deserved. Rhodes already showed his distaste in Whispers after killing your assaulter, did he not?" Adrien brushed a few of the strands stuck to my face back into the tangled mass of my hair.

"You're disgusting!" Isabelle cried, fighting against her binds. "I can't believe I ever loved you."

"Ah, you wound me." Adrien's smile was wicked as his hand moved to my chin and tilted my head to meet his gaze. "Now. Josselyn, love. Which one of your new companions would you like to watch die first?"

"Don't do this," I begged. "Just let them free and I'll stay here with you as long as you wish."

"I already gave you that chance and you failed me," he reprimanded me like a child. "And trust me, after they're gone, I *will* use you as long as I wish"

I felt hopeless and lost. I couldn't watch the murder of my lovers happen all over again. I couldn't let Adrien continue his horrible trade. Dozens of escape scenarios raced through my mind, all of them useless. Adrien would get his way again and there was nothing I could do.

"It's alright, my lady, I can choose for you." He took the blade and approached Cyprus, looking at him piteously. "Perhaps you should have learned to stop touching other people's things."

Cyprus gazed up at Adrien, a sardonic smile playing at his bloodied lips. The look in his eyes was stubborn and wild. "And you, my lord, should have learned to tie better knots."

With the speed and grace of a dancer, Cyprus rose to his feet, restraints falling to the floor. Seizing the wrist holding the knife, Cyprus twisted it behind Adrien's back as he swept his leg behind Adrien's feet. Cyprus used the weight of his body to trip Adrien backward over his leg. Adrien's head collided with the edge of the table as he went to the floor. Cyprus' hand came free, holding the knife. He leaned a knee into Adrien's chest and spared him one final thought.

"Your name will die with you, Lord Markov."

Cyprus never gave him the chance to fight back. Without hesitation or remorse, he drew the blade across Adrien's throat.

Isabelle closed her eyes and shrunk away from the scene as the blood drained from the wound.

I couldn't help but watch with morbid fascination. This man had taken everything from me. I watched the light leave his eyes. At his death I felt…nothing.

"Cyprus." I couldn't steady my voice. I needed to know he was okay.

He cut my wrists from their bonds and gently guided me to the floor.

"Cyprus…you…are you…?"

"Shhh, let's leave this place first. Then we can talk." When he turned I finally saw the long gash on his back.

Adrien hadn't cut Cyprus' hands—he'd just hurt him enough to extort Cyprus' name from me.

"Your back—" I reached for him but he made his way to Isabelle, freeing her from her ties.

"I'll be alright. I've had worse." He managed a weak smile and helped Isabelle to her feet.

"I can't believe…I can't…" Isabelle gasped and clung to him.

I lifted myself up off the ground once feeling returned to my hands. My head and body ached, begging me to rest. But Cyprus was right, we needed to leave.

"Do you think those men will still be out there?" I asked, remembering Finn and Isaac.

"Who knows how long we've been in here," Isabelle replied, her voice still shaking. "They've probably been paid and gone."

"Let me go first," Cyprus offered.

I moved toward them and took Isabelle's hand. We leaned against each other while Cyprus went to the door to secure our path.

"We're…outside," he said.

"What?" I asked dumbly.

Isabelle and I made our way to the door, avoiding the pool of blood that encircled Adrien. The first pieces of daylight glowed on the horizon and an expanse of grass separated us from the estate.

"We're in the back of the house," Isabelle murmured. "We need help. I'm going to get us help. Stay here."

We stepped out of the estranged building and closed the door. I could only hope the area stayed as isolated as it seemed. Cyprus and I watched as Isabelle ran back toward the basement. Without warning my body crumpled onto the ground and Cyprus was there to cushion my fall. Sobs wracked my entire being and He drew me close, wincing slightly as he pulled at the gash in his back. His arms were warm against my naked skin and he murmured sweet assurances while I grieved. For Jeremi and Victoria. For Cyprus and Isabelle. For myself.

XXIV

Isabelle returned to us with both Sam and his wife, Melody. They asked very few questions beyond Cyprus' name and where he hailed from. I assumed Isabelle explained our situation as the first thing Melody did was cover me in a thick cloak and wrap me in a tight hug. We were rushed to their small home near the estate while the rest of the city slept. Sam retrieved our horses while Melody tended to Cyprus' wounds and prepared all three of us hot baths, one at a time. When Sam returned, they set to work fixing us a hearty meal and I gave Isabelle enough gold to fetch us all clothing to travel in.

"Sam, if you and Melody would be interested in moving to Anastas, I'd be happy to give you both work," Cyprus stated as we ate.

"We wouldn't have anywhere to live. My family's house is far too small to take us both in." The disappointment in Sam's voice was unmistakable.

"I can take care of that as well. Really, it's the least I can do." Cyprus smiled

"We may take you up on that, m'lord. We've been talking about a little one and well…we'd love to live in a bigger city." The excitement on Sam's face warmed my heart.

"I'd be more than happy to accommodate that."

Isabelle returned with clothing and threw the pack of gold I gave her back to me.

"Edmund said he'd put it on Adrien's tab." Her face was carefully blank.

I didn't push the issue.

We dressed, but as we were readying to leave, Sam and Melody both demand we rest for a time. If not for the health of our minds, but for Cyprus' wounded back. The three of us barely fit on Sam and Melody's bed—but by that point, I could have slept in a linen closet.

They woke us a good time later. My whole body ached worse than before, my head still throbbed. But we had to leave before word of Adrien's disappearance left Valford.

Melody made us each a care package filled with food and refilled our water skins. We exchanged farewells and we were off to the Capital. Our horses were thankfully more rested than the three of us.

"I didn't get a chance to get into Adrien's documents…I just have the contract. I wish we had more." I was worried it wasn't enough. That we made the entire journey for nothing and soon Garret Rhodes would be tracking us like a hunter.

"Who said we don't?" Isabelle held up a folded paper with a broken seal in her hand. "Bailiff Garret Rhodes' seal. The contents confirm the time and date he planned to dispatch the entire Terryn family. I delivered this to Adrien two weeks before it happened and he left it in a coat pocket in his wardrobe."

"Isabelle…you may have just saved us all." I sighed in relief.

"Now to present what we have and pray," Cyprus said. "Hopefully someone's listening."

It seemed someone *was* listening. Isabelle was the one to present our documentation to the barrister and Cyprus helped fill in the few missing gaps to the story of the Terryn estate. I stood in as a witness to all of it, but my opinion wasn't viewed as valid, despite being the one purchased and sold. Within a few days' time, there were warrants out for the arrest of Bastion Rochefort, Garrett Rhodes, and Adrien Markov. Word of their corruption spread like wildfire. The Temple of Elwyn lost its good name throughout Rhoryn, forcing many of its places of worship to close their doors, and the auction house in the City of Ends was destroyed.

Garrett Rhodes was tried and found guilty of murder, treason, and misuse of his station among a myriad of other charges. He was sentenced to death and hanged as a warning to other high-ranking officials. Bastion Rochefort was found guilty of acting as an accomplice to Rhodes and Markov. They stripped him of his titles and possessions, excommunicated him from the faith, and locked him away in a cell to repent for the rest of his mortal days. Adrien Markov was never found. It was assumed he fled the continent. Those of us who knew never said a word against it.

All of this we gleaned from travelers while we rebuilt our lives in Anastas.

"You cheated! You're cheating!" Isabelle threw her cards on the table. Despite her harsh words, her laughter echoed against the walls.

"My lady, I would never!" Cyprus looked at her as if he was never more offended in his life.

"The skirt next, love. You promised." I smiled wickedly, taking a small sip of wine. We still had so many bottles to get through, but we had all evening.

"Bullshit card game. Both of you have the upper hand." Isabelle finished her glass, then stood and slipped her skirts off, revealing black, lacy underthings. She'd already lost her socks and top.

"It's called *Finan* darling and you have to think quicker than that." Cyprus poured her a new glass of wine.

"Neither of you has lost so much as a sock!" she retorted.

"Just keep at it, it'll get easier." I took her hand and squeezed it. My eyes drifted to the intricate tattoo that encircled her ring finger.

Our Isabelle. My Ring.

"Alright, but if either of you still has a shirt on in the next three hands, I'm tearing them off myself!" Isabelle declared.

"Then we'd better get serious!" Cyprus snickered.

I loved them both with all of my heart.

No one lost. No one forgotten.

Tere L'etai.

EPILOGUE

In the fairy tales I've enjoyed since childhood, Happily Ever After is always so abrupt and sudden. The prince saves the princess, they return to the castle, the king bestows his blessing, they marry, and it ends. Happily Ever After. Thankfully, mine was so much more than that.

A few years following Isabelle's Ring ceremony, Cyprus made a special trip to Lorelyn. He wanted to visit his parents and collect a few items he left behind in his hurry to Anastas. I remembered when Victoria made her travels to Lorelyn; each one took her three weeks minimum due to the nature of the journey. Isabelle and I both missed Cyprus immensely and wanted to surprise him when he came home.

The evening before his return, we devised the perfect trap. Barring the fact our devious plans were made over a few bottles of wine, Cyprus would never know what hit him. Early the next morning we made a brief run into the city, purchasing the few articles we needed. When we returned, Lily helped us put together a dinner fit for a king.

"You've really improved at cooking, Lily," Isabelle marveled.

"It's much easier when your teacher isn't yelling at you all the time." Lily stuck her tongue out at Isabelle and ducked below her playful swat.

"'Don't upset the woman preparing your food,'" I laughed, quoting a line Hilde reserved for her bawdiest of patrons.

The three of us carried the trays filled with all different manners of treats to the master bedroom. We brought a section of the dining room table in and covered it in a red, silken tablecloth for just the occasion.

"Lily, why don't you take the rest of the evening to yourself? Go out and have some fun." I handed her a small purse of coins and she took them happily.

"Thank you, m'lady." She curtsied and left the room.

"It was sweet of you to employ her," Isabelle remarked while we arranged the trays.

"I couldn't let her burn water all by herself in Valford for the rest of her life. Besides, it seems like her instructor's lightened up on her a little." I grinned and Isabelle rolled her eyes.

"Shove off. Not everything can be taught with a gentle hand."

"Clearly." I laughed and Isabelle sighed. Out of the corner of my eye, I caught the smile that tugged at her lips.

I carefully unfolded the attire we chose for the evening. During our shopping, we elicited a few sidelong glances from the clothier, but he couldn't argue with gold.

"I'm…going to need help tying this." I turned the sheer fabric over in my hands.

Isabelle had ultimately made the final say on what we would wear and I could barely see how we put them on.

She snickered and closed the door. "Must I do everything for you, Josselyn?" Closing the space between us, she unlaced my top with practiced fingers.

"I think I can undress mysel—" My words were cut short by her lips on mine.

She tugged the fabric down, taking my skirts with it and in mere moments left me standing naked and vulnerable.

I quivered beneath her touch, moving to undress her in the same fashion.

Catching my wrists, she pulled away from me. "Put your dress on," she instructed.

"You…are a terrible tease," I breathed and shivered.

Isabelle knew exactly what she'd done. "And you love me for it." She disrobed and reached for the second dress.

"That I do." I smiled. I managed to find my way through the tangle of lace that somehow passed as clothing.

Isabelle laced the back of hers first before turning her attentions to mine. Nearly everything about the outfits was identical—except hers was black and mine white. The material clung to our curves, creating floral patterns against our skin that seemed painted on rather than worn. They cut short right at the tops of our thighs, barely hiding what was underneath. Isabelle looked stunning, wearing hers with absolute confidence. I wanted to tear it off of her.

"You'll have to wait a little longer, love." She traced my jaw with her fingertips and tipped my gaze to hers. She read me like a book. "Stand up straight, don't be shy. You look magnificent."

I took her advice and set my shoulders back. I didn't have anything to hide from her or Cyprus—I shouldn't be embarrassed.

She released her hair from its traditional bun, the curls flowing around her shoulders like fire lapping at her skin.

I loosed my mane from its ties and let it fall to my waist. We donned our jewelry and touched our eyes and lips with color.

We uncorked two bottles of wine and poured our glasses full, one extra for Cyprus. Isabelle and I positioned ourselves sitting on either end of the table. Everything was set just as we devised. We shared in light conversation, sipping on the wine when Cyprus opened the door.

"Welcome home," we greeted in unison.

Stunning Cyprus was rare. Leaving him speechless never happened. The look on his face and his wandering eyes said we achieved both.

"This is…not at all what I was expecting." He gaped. He placed his travel bags on the floor and closed the door behind him. "You two have been busy."

I wanted so badly to run to him and hold him in my arms and I was sure Isabelle shared my sentiments. It seemed like years since I'd seen his handsome face and burning blue eyes. But we had a plan and I would hold back.

"You've had a long trip and we wanted to surprise you." Isabelle moved from the table to his side.

I followed suit, standing on his opposite side and handing him a glass of wine. I breathed him in; scents of rain, dust, and cinnamon wafted from his skin. "We missed you." I kissed his throat.

His skin warmed beneath my lips as he looked back and forth from Isabelle to me.

"You have no idea," he purred, kissing us one at a time.

I clutched the fabric of his tunic tightly in my hand.

Isabelle placed her cool fingers over mine, catching my gaze. *Wait.*

"You must be famished." Isabelle took his hand and led him toward the table.

"That's definitely one way to put it," he replied, his eyes never settling.

"Dinner first, then dessert." I laughed, pushing him to sit at the table.

"Lily must have been at this all day," Cyprus noted, realizing there was actually food in the room.

"Of course we helped her." Isabelle pouted. "And Josselyn gave her the night off."

"And everyone else, I hope," he murmured.

"Maybe." Isabelle and I giggled.

Despite the obvious distractions, we shared a wonderful meal together. Cyprus regaled us with tales of his family and neighbors. He was well-liked in Lorelyn and his stories said as much. His long travels proved uneventful. Though, one evening he said he met an overzealous minstrel who would sing lewd little tunes for drinks. Cyprus bought him so many that the lyrics were barely coherent and the words didn't rhyme. The entire tavern was in tears by the end of the night. The whole trip sounded incredible, but I was elated to have him back home at my side. Once we finished eating, Cyprus refilled our wine glasses.

"So, I have a few ideas, but it seems the two of you have more." He leaned back in his chair.

"We do," Isabelle replied, giving me a small nod. "Josselyn brought it up while you were gone, actually."

"Did she?" He looked at me curiously. "And what would that be?"

We stood and cleared off the table of the trays, leaving only the red cloth. From beneath it, I pulled a long, black length of fabric.

"You see, Cyprus, I have…this theory." I smirked as Isabelle seated herself in his lap, reaching her arms around his neck. "I think you always like to be in control."

I pulled the fabric over his eyes and tied it tightly behind his head, blinding him. Isabelle's mouth met his and I traced his ear with my tongue.

He moaned and shivered beneath our touch.

"We want to see what happens when you don't," I whispered.

She grabbed at his tunic and yanked it over his head. I unhooked the choker I wore and clasped it around his throat, connecting the gold chain I used as a bracelet to the front.

"Gods I've missed you both," he growled, reaching for Isabelle.

I caught his wrists, pulling his hands away from her.

"We're not done until we're satisfied," Isabelle said. She took the chain and tugged on it for him to follow. "Understand?"

"Of course, my lady." He smiled.

She grabbed him by the shoulders and forced his back against the table. I moved his arms above his head and pulled him backward so he lay down on the silken cloth. She then shifted his legs onto the surface as I fished out a pair of cuffs from beneath and hooked them around his wrists. I'd previously attached a length of rope from the cuffs to the table legs.

As I watched him struggle against the bindings, I was satisfied with my handiwork. "Couldn't have you escaping so easily."

"You thought this through," Cyprus said under his breath.

Isabelle unfastened his trousers and all but tore them off of him. "Dessert is served," she announced.

My Happily Ever After.

SPECIAL THANKS TO:

To all of my readers: I relive this story through you every time you read it and tell me what you've seen. Writing has always been my passion, but seeing my worlds through your view became my strength. Thank you so much.

Marlena Mozgawa: My fantastic cover artist and dear friend, thank you for your patience and bringing my characters to life. Thank you for my beautiful coffee mugs and gooseberry jelly.

Chris: Thank you for pointing out logical errors and things I missed my first eight times through. Thank you for playing video games with me while I pulled my hair out.

Pete: My best friend, writing companion and biggest fan. I can never thank you enough for the support you've given me throughout this entire journey of both writing and life. Thank you always for your incredible advice and suggestions.

Shelly: Thank you for threatening to kidnap me and chain me to a desk so I would keep writing. For reading this out loud at Easter dinner. My favorite cousin and best cheerleader.

Mom and Dad: Thank you for supporting my writing ever since I could pick up a pencil. For telling me, as soon as I wrote something longer than five pages, that I should keep going no matter what. For giving me your honest opinion on my intrigue, and not just my romance.

Luke: For accepting these characters as they are, even in its 2014 inception. You have truly been there from the beginning and encouraged me to keep writing. Your voice has lent so much personality to this story that it wouldn't be the same without you.

Ryan: As a fellow writer, you've helped me go through this and polish it to completion. You opened my eyes to things about these characters I never considered and forced me to look at them more deeply. Here's to many more books from both of us!

Natsuki: For editing for me at all hours of the night, helping me come up with descriptions, and acting as my graphic designer for the covers. All of this for the small price of raspberry cheese croissants and McDonald's breakfast.

Catherine LaCroix is the author of multiple award-winning fantasy stories, including *The Whispers of Rings, Little Treasures,* and *The Silent Note*. She resides in Glendale, Arizona with her four rabbits and a seemingly never-ending stock of wine. Connect with her through **www.whispersfromcat.wordpress.com** or e-mail her at **whispersfromcat@gmail.com**